CW00864166

Angling for SEA TALES *over* A HAUNTED WRECK

GILBERT SPRAUVE

Order this book online at www.trafford.com
or email orders@trafford.com

Most Trafford titles are also available at major online book retailers.

Print information available on the last page.

ISBN: 978-1-4907-9334-4 (sc)
ISBN: 978-1-4907-9333-7 (hc)
ISBN: 978-1-4907-9338-2 (e)

Library of Congress Control Number: 2019931678

Trafford rev. 02/23/2019

www.trafford.com

North America & international
toll-free: 1 888 232 4444 (USA & Canada)
fax: 812 355 4082

Angling for SEA TALES *over* A HAUNTED WRECK

Pssst, Reader:

If *to angle for* is mainly *to watch for,* or even *to wait for,* then beware of ads that promise "the perfect or compleat angler." Such an entity simply does not exist! Besides, when you've set aside the question of *how* you angle, there lingers that of *where* you do it. Not to mention *when* to *quit!*

That much said:

Caribbee Kraal is the way some older ocean maps named what we now call the Caribbean Sea or Basin. It is also worth noting that "bossal" meant during that same period "unseasoned African." (Their "seasoned" brothers and sisters, mimicking their masters, would shamelessly speak of them as they often do to this day as "saltwater Negros.")

Also, in our traditions, "at the crossroads" is our cultural haven—be it on sea or land. Our more esteemed culture bearers counsel respect and for spaces bearing that name; likewise, for all that falls within our cultural *kraal.*

So, it was that the vessel Bossal Snare toted its share of issues before putting out to sea on this week-end fishing trip. And, below its waterline, it could certainly do without that untimely collision with a playful whale shark for the trip to gain its share of notoriety!

Nor did its skipper, Ton-Ton-Da-Da, need a bruising and eventually losing hand-line battle with that miscreant of a certain cross fish, given the stressful task already on his mind of managing the gang of cheeky and often roguish pan-Caribbean mates that made up his crew. [And, let it be known even this early: That this certain know-it-all crew member they called in patois—and for good reason—"Samwekadiw" [francophone Creole for "What-did-I-tell-you!"], would dare to side with the monster malicious fish and explain the why and how of its foul deed when it dislodged the anchor of the by-then disabled vessel to set it adrift in the wide Caribbean Kraal! Possessing mastery, *he* claimed, of deep-sea fish wisdom, simply because *he'd* fished the great depths near *his* home island, and none present matched that background in real life experience! Choops! And Tsk, tsk!]

But, with SamwekadiW [And the reader is begged to bear with these untimely intrusions. Further on it will be seen that they are ascribed to some uncontrollable narrational babbling that is then explained as "effervescence."], when it was his turn—after backing off on the theme back-to-life tales—he spun a most frightful story that started out with a red planet emitting a band of machete-bearing warriors pursuing him the lone wolf night fisherman and ending with an undersea confrontation at a haunted wreck between him and a colossal congo eel.

But the storytelling might be getting ahead of itself at this point!

CONTENTS

THE VESSELS

Bossal Snare

Dixie Island Girl (DIG)

Enforcer(s) Patrol provocateurs and Pursuit cruisers/chasers

THE CREW

Ton-Ton-Da-Da, Skipper and Part Owner of Bossal Snare

The Major-in-Retirement, long-time buddy of Ton-Ton, partner-owner (not on board for this trip)

Ras Reb (aka Rusta), youngest member, Pan-African-to-the-bone

Patate Mama-W (aka **SamwekadiW**), deep-water Windward Island "certified" fisherman

State-of-Mind, Afro-American wannabe West Indian homey, fix-all tech

Black Mole, retired Fire sergeant turned fisherman, neighbor of Ton-Ton Da-Da

Red Bone, apprentice sexton, neighbor of Ton-Ton Da-Da and "seke-bem-bem" to Black Mole

THE TAKES

Skipper Ton-Ton Da-Da: "No Preaching, no Judging!"

Ras Reb: "Pan-African, etc." Bossalism avatar

Patate-Mama-W or SamwekadiW: Champion of "The Depths"

State-of-Mind: "Ain' no Mountain . . . or Ocean, etc."

Black Mole: "Burn the Trash; ban the Plastics!" or "I say one . . ."

Red Bone: "Ban' yo' belly, Ben!" also ". . . to say two!"

THE PLACES

"Long de Bay," (sometimes) with "Sudge" brewing

The Tourist Liner Dock

Homeport in the Careenage

Unda de Cyalm

De Broddas, or Monkey Roost

The Strait between 2 West Africa-named cays

In the Caribbean Kraal (adrift)

Haven, Unda de fabled Mango Tree

THE MANTRAS

Yabba-pot-a-yabba;

Time—take it, or tic it

TWO FACES OF A HIGH SEA!

"G**ound Sea"** (or "Sudge") it's called, and mariners' womenfolk in these parts (with toddlers mimicking them), at its mere specter, holler its name woefully and in despair! It rolls in during late autumn, several weeks after the laughing gulls (having encroached on the "Who? You!!!" gull the whole bothersome mating-and-nesting summer) have now gone back north or south, "*or wherever they came from in the first place!!!*"

Long period waves from northerly storms—mostly early nor'easters—are thumping the islands' exposed Atlantic-side shorelines.

Plucky young northerly men have brought their boards, and they flock to the passage between these two neighboring cays that bear the names of African peoples from the earliest European settlement period—Loango, Mingo-by-Congos-—, the channel between them further reduced and restricted by coral reefs and some derelict iron wreck, which eventually slid off one of the facing reefs and then impaled and wedged (via calcifying) itself on a median outcropping rock.

The surfing frolics of the inevitable young "snowbird-State-siders" did not find favor in the eyes of either Skipper (Maas) Ton-Ton Da-Da or Ras Reb, otherwise, consistently and visibly irreconcilable adversaries on most matters!

For the skipper these visitors' presence and their recreational pass-time meant degradation and ruination of an important back-up fishing bank for yellowtail snappers on days when the trek to the blue-water Big High Shoal was out of the question.

For Reb, youngest crew member, their activity was an irritant also, since it was further evidence of Government's blatant pro-Tourism bias, and its neglect of food-production and other grassroots subsistence priorities. "Let them take their effing boards and head back to Malibu or Santa Monica, or even Negril, if that's what Jamaicans want! (Though Maroonage and the imprimatur of Garvey and Marley on that island's mindset should safely trump such an intrusion and indignity in that place!) Jah! Put in place a ban on dese friggin' boards, wave riders an' gadgets like dem dat infec' our Jah-blessed resources and seascapes! Turn them away even at our airports and seaports!

[**yabba pot etc, etc**.]

Hmmph, not likely, wid dese puppets dat parade as Government leaders! No balls!

So, (while, further on, in the course of this account the rub between Reb and Skipper Ton-Ton Da-Da appears to have commenced with a fishhook barb, it is not insurmountable and, in fact, turns largely on a generational and *Class* divide, the skipper's age matching more that of the young man's grandparents, with his complexion being more that of their northern Recreation tormentors!

Indeed, the race and "shade" issue between them aside (along with the nagging question "*whose* earth and *whose* rights?"), Reb through residual Afro-Caribbean home-bred customs would normally address the skipper as "Uncle."

This is not to say that a certain bossal business in the naming of the boat could also be totally swept off the board!

If the skipper's buddy and partner in the boat purchase (not a true acquaintance of Reb) wanted to pull dumb stunts like mucking around in our *bossal-ness*, let him go ahead. But the old man should know better than to tolerate the disrespect!

Get this pale-skin, pudgy skipper's dander up, and he'll tell you he is "as West Indian as any friggin' man on this boat or anywhere else!"

"Oh, yeah? Prove it! Crank up your big George Forman fists an' slap de front teet' dong your forward partner's t'roat for mockin' our cultural heroes, the Bossals! An affront you yourself would never commit! At leas' not within earshot of any up an' standin' one of us Culture-wise homeboys!")

[**"Yabba- pot, etc."**]

Yet, below the surface, there was another noteworthy bond between these two shipmates, plausibly one that shadowed a brand of Spiritualism, if you looked at it from the Fishing Tradition perspective. It had to do with the freshest mash Ton-Ton-Da-Da offered the game when he chummed.

The extreme locations to which the skipper would travel to be able to offer the most delectable and pollution-free meal in the form of *mash* to his quarry were noteworthy. The very sand used for the mash! He would sail that extra three or four miles on the lumbering and quaking round-bottom "Bossal Snare" to that bay where the sand was supremely fresh and undefiled to fill up his twenty used ice bags, before heading out to the fishing banks. This care given to the quarry's food preferences matched the kosher-linked consciousness and practices of Ras Reb's I-man people as it related to their food choices and practices.

Once anchored at the bank, the skipper would set his wooden tray on the stern deck and artfully mix fresh, ice-chilled fry with fine, clean sand the way a highly decorated chef would do with his condiments and precious ingredients, taking care to separate out and discard pebbles, shells or other debris.

No matter the composition of his crew on any trip, he alone, again like one ordained into that role, performed the task of mixing and casting mash.

Now, Ton-Ton Da-Da pondered, with those Natural Resources experts (not to mention their chums in Tourism, the Park and the Chamber), just try to break out this process, yeah, the same folks that credential these snowbird surfers to frig-up my life! Just try, especially in a public hearing or charrette. See how far you get before Mr. Chair raps the gavel and announces "Non-germane!" Or, "**Time**, for the last time, Testifier!" Or "In fact, meeting recessed!"

This routine abuse of his and his folks' rights reverberates with such intensity that the skipper sees himself on his Day of Judgment—minimal practicing Catholic that he is—gaveled into an absolutely muted, senseless and pulverized mass of compliance (*despite the promise made to us, from the Pulpit and the Politician's Podium of a mind of our own, so we could and should be free thinkers!*)

Yet, there was still this other gripe the skipper harbored; it had to do with an initial encounter and recurring ones between his Bossal Snare and a tour vessel bearing the name Dixie Island Gal or DIG. **[Time, take it or tick it!]**

WELCOME . . . AHOY!

(**That** was the greeting the tourist client read on the cover of the *Island Intro and Guide* stacked on the dockside counter by where the DIG and the Snare docked and operated from.)

The touring visitor reads the above and naturally wants to know more about the character, etc. of the Master of the vessel. The latter will in turn respond to any inquisitive poking, that he is like any other *real local* captain, and the visitor's attention might better be employed in observing his crew! He will add that he is "no referee" to the sustained banter and jousting between his ever-chatty crew that takes place on board. "But, yo' free to lissen in; might learn one or two t'ings 'bout how we live!'

Even so, the Master, who is also part-owner of the Snare, by his thunderous voice and voluminous presence, maintains a degree of order throughout the running taunts and the many attempts at defiance against his stated rules of conduct which, simply stated are: "No Preaching, no Judging! Period!"

Besides, in some respects he selects his crew with a view towards balance, and for this trip has these two older allies—neighborhood mates.

In the meantime, as it says further on the cover and guide stacked on the dockside counter:

"A Special Welcome to the BBP#1 or Boarding Briefing Pier#1! To the right, all Pleasure-Seekers and Fun-struck Adult *Swim*mers! To the left, all certified Global Culture Consortium, (GCC) Associates and Visiting Preservationists!

Promotional Orientations (PROMO-O) commence fifteen minutes sharp before departure. You may board and visit briefly one of two vessels, as suits your fancy. Furthest to your right, *Dixie Island Gal*, the bling-bling, tourist ferry, festooned in patriotic streamers, once and past tender to a Gulf oil rig. Docked furthest to my right, The *Bossal Snare,* the famously cranky, round-bottom fishing vessel, most recently documented in the New Concord Maritime Registry as a blue-water lobster boat, earlier logged as a scrub-hauler of seines in the Gulf of Guinea.

(Visitors coming aboard the Bossal are advised to exercise extra caution against slipping and tripping, as the vessel is in preparation for her regular fishing trip at the drop-off, and the deck is wet and slippery.)

Pssst: Permission to board this vessel was only granted moments ago, and the key concession was linked to the visiting crowd getting a chance to see "what these small fishing fleets are up against!" (It's the kind of two-faced dealings that slick technocrats in our island Administration can fashion with the snap of a finger! No one familiar with the workings of pork-barrel politics needs a road map for the details of this type of transaction. The outcome supposedly adds cultural flavor and a tinge of "rusticity" to the visitor's experience!)

Trouble selecting which boat to visit?

Our unbiased advice: Barely drop in on the crew of this craft, the Bossal Snare! West Indian men from several islands in the chain (with at least one with *claims* to such links), preparing for a typical weekend fishing trip.

No, you will not physically continue *on board* the Snare, but, instead, after acquainting yourself with the captain and crew, hearing a sampling of their tales and experiencing their surroundings, you will, in time, through news clippings, various eye-witness reports, on-board logs, diaries, journals and the like, available in collected personal papers of the co-owner (for the more research-inclined), likely share in, appropriate and even expand on what took place with the Bossal's master and crew during this weekend fishing trip.

Appropriate and *expand*, because, dear reader, those privileges fall within your rights! After all, through whatever means, you have in hand the text. You're about to strain your eyes and your imagination following the many twists and turns of the events and tales therein contained. Why not exercise your rights!

[To be honest, the recommendation above—about the vessel to visit— was not exactly objective! While not an ideal Caribbean culture melting pot—or hornets-nest—, this choice offers close-up glimpses into the *Pell-Mell* of our volatile co-habitation on these islands!]

This trip takes place on a Friday full moon night just days short of Christmas. The crew customarily know enough about each other, during lulls occasioned by the slackening of the current and/or disinterest on the part of the presumptive sea-life game, to engage in verbal jousts, made up mostly of tales and loose accounts—some of them, verily, of dubious veracity—of events lived and fancied.

DOMINOS PRELUDING TO THE CROSSROADS EVENT

Now then . . .(scooping from an on-land "man-betta-man" scenario), as if the poor lighting wasn't enough of a gripe for the domino players, the sidewalk leading up to the entrance of the supermarket is barely 3 feet wide, and the evening shoppers, at a certain point, are squeezing by each other even more tightly as they go about their week-end commerce with the establishment.

For, with the setting of the sun, the regulars have arrived, claimed their space with folding chairs and a low wooden roll-out table whose top is a draught board, though it serves well for domino games.

Here, against the klakking and slapping of the white black-spotted domino bones, and to the gentle lapping of the wind-driven ripples against the nearby waterfront bulkhead's rusted studs, they argue about a certain "BLACKOUT" business.

"You gon' tell me how it staat, YOU?" [KLAK]

[**Yabba pat a-yabba**]

The Bookish Spectator [while stealthily withdrawing to a safer place]: "I only tellin' it how I hear an' read it."

"How you *manage' to* hear an' read it! [klak-slap] Mister, I don't deal with how I hear an' read not'ing, no-friggin'-t'ing! I deal wid what I know! [klak]. Fact! . . . an', what I know is: [**Watch out, Miss! Hold your bags higher, before yo' tumble de bone-dem off de board as yo' make yo' way tru! An' w'ile yo' at it, Miss, excuse me language to dis friggin' book-slave, Miss!**] As I was sayin: ***I*** it is who confirm fo' him de name BLACKOUT! ***I*** who do dat! OK? Now, you an' all present, ready to hear how it staat?"

Now, (in his mind, at least), having crushed and scattered the competition, our dominant (alpha!) domino player, in presumably full control of his audience, proceeded to lay bare a relates about a would-be forerunner of "BLACKOUT," a man who had returned from the Second World War shell-shocked (though few of the locals even knew the expression at that time) and who then made it a habit of daily appearing on Main Street, posing in such military decking—including leggings—as he still possessed or could beg or borrow, to parade erectly and with great flair, while sounding off and complying with self-commands of "Forward, march!," "To the right; to the left; about face . . . etc."

"Dat man people at fus called 'Air-raid,'" he related.

"But there was other returnin' soldiers dat carried on in ways like dat. Tryin' to keep up wid de sailors off de ships, when on shore. Dey dared to take public liberties wid decent women folk passin' wit'in deir reach!. An' I could give de full list of some of de women, includin' hi-brow society ones who didn't mine a slap on de backside from dem sailor boy!

"One of dese strange-behavin' fellows I 'member from bicycle rides to de countryside dat we, as neighborhood boys, used to take on Sunday an' holiday afternoons:

"It had dis stumpy, old White man, pale like tissue-paper an' jus' as disagreeable who always show up from nowhere when we got to de Crossroads. Older folks had warned us about strange t'ings dat took place at de Crossroads! 'An' don't let nightfall ketch yo' near dere! Alyo' mus look out fo' each odda!'

"De man used to take it upon himself to t'reaten us, claimin' he was guardin' de owner's garden or farm to stop us from praagin' w'at didn't belong to us.

"He could never tell us who de owner-dem was. Or how he know what our intention was!

"An' den, de elders tole us to never mind him; he too had been a soldier an' had 'a screw missin'. Besides, any such owner, as he claim to be guardin' for, who would deny po' town chirren de chance to pick a public mango, soursop, guava, sugar apple, mamey or mesple at de Crossroads was headed for certain damnation! He an' whoever he did his dirty work for! **He** we call Black-out numba two! Though he was White an' had straight-hair! De fus Blackout had dead an' was bury in de Danish cemetery!"

It was conduct of this sort, our dominoes boss claimed— while, with great fanfare, slapping down the double-six bone on the board— that made people brand strange-acting men, especially those on our main thoroughfares and regularly at the Crossroads, with War names like "Blackout, "Air Raid," and "All Clear."

"War is a vexation an' a plague, an' when it blossom 'tis a hundred-fold worse!" the oldest of the players declared.

All the bla-bla, however, was of no consequence! For the competing book-bred historian the domino boss was sure he had shut down re-emerged—now in the shadows for obvious personal security reasons—and hissed: "Bull! Dis man is talkin', if you listen good, mostly about himself. Himself an' individual *persons*! A common case of narrow mindedness in dis place! In odda words, he don't get it! People want to know more 'bout de Crossroads. He keeps on tellin' you, *he did dis, an' de odda one did dat*, talkin' about himself an' company! Somebody, go tell him I say dat!"

*So . . . we return to the high seas with this crossroads business! For if you didn't know it, at this very moment on this Caribbean Sea, cradle to our islands, Crossroads to four continents, a tale-telling duel is chomping at the bit. You can feel its lyrics wafting in the air and its magical syncopated contours and content are already streaming into the heads, consciousness and creativity of our pre-eminent calypsonians/griots. Hitch that bluster of yours on to our stories told so far and those to tell, Mister Boss of the boardgame! If you can't do that then hold your peace!" [**And there are expectations an' standards to uphold, for in this town at least, every member of the league of domino men is a mariner in good standing from days past!**]*

Such were the words muttered timidly and musings at a safe distance from the bullying board-game master by our retreating spectator; softly spoken words that would clear out obstructions in the cultural and archival path of our sea duel. For in like manner that rivers get dammed, so the torrent of tales will at times caulk, and will only resume its flow through forceful Effervescence-driven de-blocking!]

And this is precisely what the curbside domino game—*remotely*, it is true, but most *certainly*—did for our tale-fest!

(As for the Dixie Island Gal! Should anyone still be interested! There'll be time for her later. Besides, a chunk of (or, at least, about) her, usefully, comes through, up to the last sea saga in the present volume.)

The pacifying posture of Maas Ton-Ton, the Snare's master—neutral as he would wish it to be (for biased or bombastic he is not!)—is observed through the commanding presence carved out for him and imposed by Maritime Traditions Canons of his leadership role as Master (dare we say Buckra Master?) on the High Seas!

Yet this local autocracy ramifies more as the Master becomes increasingly suspicious of a possible lurking challenge to his dictates by the youngest of the crew, the same Afro-Caribo-centric named Reb, the one who first utters the mantra "yabba-pot-a-yabba," which is shorthand for his personal Redemption Song lyrics.

Skipper Ton-Ton Da-Da understands well the word "brave" for its sense of power and courage and when it has to do with "to act." As master of his vessel, he must always be prepared to brave the worst that Nature might cast his way. And with a crew like the current one, he needed to be alert at all times for whatever untoward act that might fill their fantasy, including a power grab! And, the outcome in either case would not be that he performed heroically.

Heroics? No! He's a practical man. (There are ways to deal with whatever might brew!)

View it as you would a boxing match—a clichéd take in matters like the one at hand! In this corner of the ring, it is Ton-Ton Da-Da and his handlers, Black Mole and Red Bone. In the opposite one you have Reb, the young Pan-Africanist, his Dominican/St. Lucian cohort, Patate-Mama-W and "slippery" State; one moment, Stateside Afro-American, the next, "bintu" West Indian!

The stage being set, the tale-swap is panting to break out! (The skipper has his lesser role to play in the row.)

"Yet an' still," there's more to this night sea adventure than fatuous tale-jousts among West Indian sea men, (widely recognized as outstanding performers in the sport.)

FROM BOARD GAME (all the way) TO SEA-MUSINGS

While folklorists almost a century ago roamed through our region collecting their quota of several dozen traditional folktales which they published in a general West Indian compendium, on our islands currently fairytales are of little interest and usually of less consequence. It could be because of the severe toll on our attention span and the need to circumscribe our harsh realities or keep them in suspense. A jumbie story here and a werewolf story there if you're thinking about the traditional setting of say a family campground or a moonlight gathering. That's about it for spinning tales! The practice loses ground in the face of the following given: where three are gathered, no less than two time-bound tales will simultaneously emerge, with each one's teller demanding the full attention of the listener; grabbing his lapel, and pinching flesh, if necessary!

And if after a contest you ask the dominant raconteur how he won out, he's likely to boast, "Anyone can defecate like a dog; it's to tremble like him while doing it!" (Piece of cultural wisdom picked up from a Guadeloupean griot!)

Some linguists and other social scientist who have studied this culture have noted a heightened tendency among members—irrespective of their overall life experiences—to present matters, characters and situations in terms of their solvency, fluidity, vaporizing, emulsifying, viscosity, etc. So, our storytellers, in depicting events and personalities when under full sail, often resort to words like slimy, slippery, droopy, pushy, mucky, greasy and the like. Not to mention: pissy-tailed, bully, frowsy and "piss-on-hot-rock-and-smellin' it."

Fortunately, cases of such excesses are of rare frequency in what follows.

SEA FORCES FROLICKING AT FOREDAY

In the wee hours before the moonset and the sunrise, the outing plummets dramatically towards a critical abyss in consequence of high drama between the Bossal's hull and what can only be described as a playful whale shark. Matters spiral even further off course and downward due to the strenuous obstinacy and resistance of another sea beast!

Reacting to the first of these encounters, Bone exclaims: "Watta t'ing. . ." and Mole finishes:

". . . to tell de King!" (For their call/response buttressed by the "I say *one* to say *two*" conversational extender is so deeply ingrained that they often spontaneously complete each other's thoughts and utterances.

Was shark mentioned? If indeed the sea beast was in the neighborhood! Playful or willful, the skipper and Reb, otherwise adversaries to the bone, would cut him no slack!

For here these two found themselves on common turf, haunted by nothing less than the specter of the on-land *sharking* they'd had to navigate, each in his own way, to eventually escape from the political gauntlet they, as "rookies" had been made to run in an earlier life

(This whale shark event (pre-announced to the reader in the opening pages of this report) where the sea beast thumped the Snare below the waterline "in her bread basket," took place shortly after the tale swap began. So, while the rest of the crew were by then in tongue-in-cheek mode the skipper and young Reb could only confront the stark reminder of the sharking that had victimized them in an earlier life.)

"Did I not pay up my dues before moving onto the sea?" each one mused.

BARELY A SPECK

These week-end fishing trips aboard Ton-Ton Da-Da's cranky Bossal Snare sometimes took an unpredictable turn. For this reason, Reb was often of two minds, up to the last moment, when he got the message: on Friday afternoon they would meet at the lagoon dock.

By the time Ton-Ton Da-Da docked the Snare, he would have spent most of the daylight hours hunting fry in bays half-way around the island and in inlets at nearby cays.

His success or frustration in pursuing the fry bait these recent times often molded—even more so than *which side of the bed he got out on*—his disposition by the time he encountered his crew.

As for today, it looked like the past half-a-day hadn't been the best of times.

Yet in time the wind did drop. The sea was calm enough. The crew had boarded, and the Bossal Snare had chugged along an hour and then some the ten miles to the Big Edge also known as High Shoal.

On the way to the banks Mole had established his singular importance to this trip by relating to the others how close they had come to being left back on land. "Ton-Ton Da-Da rush back on board, an' right away start up de diesel; he was in a foul-arse mood, mumblin' about de Rustas, as he duz call dem, dat raid his grafted mango tree filled to de brim wid her ratoon crop, jus' las' nite. (Alyo' will rememba how Ton-Ton foreva braggin' 'bout how dat mango tree arrive on dis island as a li'l maaga an' miserable plant/slip from

Guadeloupe, how it weadda drought an' goat mout' to persevere, an' today bear such a tasty fruit.) Well, das de tree wha' de good-fo-notten-dem raid las' night. De man orda me to cyast off right away! I know he was feelin' real cross—an' dat too, as de elders tell us, would pass! So, I fidget arong wid de stern rope long enough for Ton-Ton to cool down an' fo' you fellows to scamper aboard! Cross meh heart!"

Here, Bone, Mole's on-board closest buddy and consummate reader of signs from above, clasping his hands in mock prayer invoked the Man-From-Above's merciful providence. Since in its absence, who knows what act of madness thc skipper would commit! *Out dere on de open sea wid de wrong crew!*

Little did they know it. He'd taken the extreme solution some time back, let down by a careless, tardy gang of sea mates. And the lesson learned was clear and enduring: Never again that path!

For no amount of anger or frustration would get Skipper Ton-Ton to set off for this trip again with just any scrub-hauled crew! The one experience he'd had based on a hasty crewing decision still counseled temperance and level-headed action.

On that day, unable to resist the urge for the hunt once he'd learned from a reliable source that the hardnose jacks were running, he'd hurriedly made the hire of two unknowns.

Well. . . not exactly unknowns!

The scoop, "hardnose runnin'" came with a tip-off on how he could quickly muster a low-budget crew. So, Skipper Ton-Ton had prowled and poked around in the guts of the port sector, then on the beach, and finally taken on as mates two American beach vagrants to then set out for the high shoal banks.

On any regular fishing day and with a crew of regulars there are those moments during the long haul to the banks, when at the helm Maas Da-Da silently lays out his plan for the hunt: a study of the currents and the weather conditions, a review in his mind of the tackle he has prepared; the "guinging" (snelling) wire, the size of the hooks, the chum and the bait on hand, including the always handy fresh fry for sprinkling on the surface should bonito and tuna make their appearance at the bank.

A born fisherman's mind is like that. Those who don't know better might call it "sea dreaming!"

So, while at the helm, he had slipped into his reverie of fast and furious action from the feisty hardnose. "Blap, Plop, Plap," as the catch landed. This time, however, his thoughts ended abruptly!

For . . . enter his motley two wacky mates, the pair of vagrants he'd hurriedly mustered as crew!

In short order he would learn how rudely inquisitive the two beachside hires were. Clearly more than he'd bargained for! Simple service hands to simply cast the anchor and pull it when ordered! Plus, should the action heat up, you pass each one a hand line with a warning to watch out for entanglements that could entail loss of a section of a finger or a toe. The rest he could handle by himself!

Clearly, he wasn't prepared for the barrage of trip-hammer distracting queries the two cast his way, which he could only fend off with typical West Indian taciturn monosyllabic grunts. (Our cooks are expert at this tactic, deployed against those strangers or guests—usually from the north—who barge their way into our kitchens to sniff out and mine centuries-old culinary treasures.)

Caged-in at the helm of the vessel, the skipper found himself under siege by these pesky drifters he had hastily recruited!

And after a while the two discovered that the effective tactic against the skipper's petulant disposition was through mutism of another kind, namely exclusion.

That's when the communication tug-of-war took a different turn.

So, having gained the upper hand, eventually (since they were two to his one), they would block him out and begin their private prattle, consisting mostly of a string of jabs at locals and local culture.

Skipper Ton-Ton Da-Da, after a few minutes, noticed that his mates, when it worked for them, viewed him as kith and kin. No doubt, this was based on similar skin hue. (Did they know that precisely that kind of stereotyping, applied in reverse, in their older years, would automatically ostracize them—and even him—and get them all called "werewolf" by unruly youngsters?)

So, after uttering one vicious slander after another against everything and every soul local, they were now casting about for agreement from their captive skipper. To make matters worse, whatever they were using before boarding was now taking full effect, especially on the taller one.

At one point, Jerry, the tall one, begins singing the way the skipper had heard him do on the beach, "This beach is my bitch . . ." (only, now, in the second verse, he replaced "beach" with "boat," which woke up his sidekick who had started to doze off his booze.)

So, how did I get here? Maas Da-Da asked himself. Yet he knew well the answer!

For a born fisherman, the quest after the next *bigger catch* will, at every instant, turn into the compulsive gambler's last desperate crap shoot. So when, late that afternoon, he got news that the hardnose were running on his favorite bank, he put it in his head that crew or no crew he was joining the fête! *Plain and simple, that's how I got here! Must I lay bare how, in a cold sweat and my head reeling from the visions of finding the bank of hardnose and making a killing, "flap-blap-plap," as they landed in the boat . . . I let myself be seduced with the following bright idea from a non-seagoing acquaintance:*

"You need a standby crew? (For I know how hard it could be, tryin' to round-up your regulars on such short notice!) It got dese two nuisance 'come-here-as-tourists-an'-won't-leave' camping out on de beach! Just hook up wid dem before dey get bline drunk, like dey duz do by noon every day. When yo' done wid dem, drop dem off on somebody else's beach . . . wherever!"

(Had this informer been present at the critical moment of the disjuncture between skipper and standby crew, he would have uttered: "Oops! You caught them too late!" And even later in the encounter, his informer, if he could read the skipper's mind at this point, would call out, "Christ! I didn't mean for you to dispose of dem *dat* way!")

So now, as much as needs to be known about that encounter is known, Ton-Ton would relate to fishing colleagues afterward. But wait! Here now is the extended report of the nonsensical jabbering between his bargain-basement crew:

"Fool! We're not on the beach! We're on the high seas! Aboard the . . . what shall we call her . . . Bride of Neptune, for crying out loud!"

"Gotcha, Buddy! Then this bride-boat ***is*** my bride-boat . . . And I . . ."

Buddy: "Shhhhsh, our skipper doesn't like where you're going with that! I see the eye he's giving you."

Jerry: Ok, then! "This ocean is my ocean, ditto. From the Virgin Islands to the Colorado Mountains . . . And I can piss the distance between them . . . And, just to prove it!" (He started to unzip.)

Buddy: "No, no! Don't! You're crossing the line . . ."

But it was too late; Jay had indeed crossed the line!

"Look good before you leap, Ton-Ton! And, another thing, if it sounds too good to be true, then . . ." and so on! Where was such good sense when I needed it, Skipper Ton-Ton Da-Da wonders?.

But the words of his on-land dealmaker kept ringing in his ears: "But, I tell you already, it have dese two fellas pitch deir tent an' sleepin' bag on de beech damn nearly six months ago; claim dey lookin' fo' sea work. Not'ing on de sea dey cyan't do! An' remember, afterwards . . . any place but here, when you're done with dem!" (Such inducements whispered yet one more time! An' me, like an idiot!)

"What yo' tellin' me! Where I go find dem?" And so, it went.

"Unda de almon' tree, nex' to de Battery gate. Mind yo'! Yo' mus' cyatch dem befo' deir booze in de mornin', an' yo' good to go! De wors' t'ing could happen to dem is ***dey go to sea an' don't come back!*** *Who go give a damn? At least de beach will be rid of dem!"*

The truth be told, Maas Da-Da initially brushed off the insinuation about dumping the continental beach bums somewhere in the open Caribbean after use. It was not in his nature to even entertain such a thought! Little does he know that soon after their "mustering" and their boarding, his tolerance and principles would be tested as never before by the arrogance, orneriness and plain racism of the two beach over-stayers.

The skipper puzzled over the fellows' behavior and attitude for a while. Then he figured it out this way: *It absolutely must have to do with de closeness of my complexion to deirs. Hell, dey're takin' me for one of deir own! Especially bein' de skipper an' owner of de vessel, etc., etc.* They'd quickly meandered into a litany of slander and defamations about "those people."

"Hell, dey're my people," Ton-Ton Da-Da thinks.

[Until . . . God forbid!]

Not to worry, Mole and Bone! An', decidedly, not to puff up wid sanctimonious significance on your skipper's nex' move!

Laughing Gull Rock has no known human inhabitant, (and that surprises no one around here! For neither do Fallen Jerusalem and Dead Man's Cay, its wind-blown kin in size and isolation. But its lighthouse keeper alights there, always alone, from a navy grey weather-beaten tug, at intervals set by dates of the equinox and the solstice.

It is at mere yards in the lee of this remote natural navigational hazard that Maas Da-Da got his riotous pair of crew mates to cast the anchor. After a hasty explanation of the practice whereby he maximized his catch by posting mates on rocks to fish with hand lines, while the remainder stayed and worked aboard, Maas Da-Da, with his cranky dinghy that he called "Rub-a-Tub," ferried ashore first one then the other of the two marginal assistants, reminding one and then the other to "look out for your mate!" (All the while mumbling: "The innocent shall pay for the guilty! Prattle on! Let's see if you can out-prattle the frigging sea birds! Try, in gull lingo, telling them how 'dis rock is my rock, etc.') And other boastful forwardness of the sort!"

That was the last he saw of them.

Though he did learn sometime later of a rescue and a resettling of the two on a cay farther down the chain.

He considered himself having kept up his part of the deal with the -man who had guided him to them. He also imagined their rescuer had some harsh sarcastic remark he himself would not have been able to resist making about the noise in their head they'd had to bear from the gulls the whole "confounded" time they'd spent on the forsaken rock! Not to mention the dive-bombing and target-practice, shitting (on their heads and even more private parts) by the same put-upon hosts during daylight and moonlit hours.

Sum total! Whatever the disgust Skipper Ton-Ton might experience with his regular crew as far as readiness and reliability, for sure, the answer could never again be raking and scraping defective drifters on our public beaches!

Worry 'bout me an' crazy ideas? I am not the one on dis vessel you should be worried about, Ton-Ton Da-Da posits.

Who else possesses the know-how I have about boats an' what dey're built of? Keel to spa an' stem to stern. I who has visited, from bayside to summit, jus' about every arable cay or island in dis chain, know de trees an' forests, de mahoganies, cypresses, gommier (excellent for plankin'), haita (wid branches dat make perfek ribs, needin' no template, adze or plane, you name it!

Did anyone hear any gibberish from me 'bout tinkin' wida or higha dan oddas?

Jus' a hint!

ABOUT AN OIL-SLICK MOON-GLOW VIGIL

SO . . . now, it was up to the moon.

Its fore-glow was but a speck—hardly more than a dot—on the burnished line where sea and sky merge. And as it pierced the murky horizon the curvature that peeked through the sea-borne line of clouds during its lazy, yet foreboding ascent was already more sickle-shaped than precisely rounded.

Lazy because by contrast the south tide which in this region is closely espoused to the moonrise had been particularly hasty in presenting itself and drawing the Bossal-Snare over the oil-like placid sea taut against its anchor painter. *Foreboding* because, if a crimson sunset around here reliably portends storms from the west the following morning, then a gloomy moonrise promised a certain unspecified tumult—many see-saw tossing moments for the Snare and crew once the anchor-killick was firmly set on the sand and coral bottom at the fishing bank. "*Pink clouds in the evening; mariners' warning for the next morning!*" Or something like that!!!

[Skipper Ton-Ton Da-Da had a piece of advice for crew members who would bitch about the Snare's round-bottom rolling while anchored during high seas and adverse winds. "If you know nottin' about hull shapes under rough sea conditions like dese, den daag betta dan you! Grumble about de tossin' an' rollin' of dis craft much as you want! Blame her bottom fo' de tossin'! One hull design you don't want, is dat of de gangling Danish steamer/trader a fella bought 'cheap,' so he believe, an' put to run routes in dese parts. So . . . run yo' mout' on dis round-bottom vessel as much as you want; she go tilt to port, she go come back an' dip to starboard, an' so fort'. De long Danish steamer I'm talking about, hmmph, she tilt an' then she tumble one time! Which is what happen one Christmas trip a few years ago. Wid loss of a total precious cargo an' all but two lucky mates! An' if dat don't convince yo' to stop criticizin' de rollin' of dis boat in de seas, try to remember w'at de ole folks say about de skinny white egret—which we call de gyaalin—an' de cow: Yo' don't stan' on cow back and tell her she ugly!"]

During these first minutes of the moonrise, the tide being slack-to-light the fishermen in busying themselves the better to prove their worth to their boss turned to the task of inspecting their hand lines against bee-nests, hard kinks and slipshod splices.

In doing this, you drew thirty or so yards at a time off your yo-yo hand reel, curling the monofilament in even loops of about a foot and a half in diameter onto the nearest flat surface, pausing along the way to attend to any pesky irregularity and stretching the line tight, every 15 feet or so, in order that a larger fish that might attack your bait could be paid without fuss the line due it for the long haul.

Reb, younger than anyone else on board—and a shade darker in complexion than even Black Mole— in these moments of collective and intense anticipation often fished for a rebuke for the infraction of stealthily—which is to say behind Ton-Ton's back—filing down the barb off his hooks.

Now, in matters of people's personal choices, the Skipper was not one to pass judgment. With one or two exceptions!

In fact, he never missed a chance to broadcast his disdain for judges and priests. (And, it was in your interest not to go scriptural in pleading the case for them in his court; he didn't flinch and could chew you up and spit you out instantly.) "Every serious human conflict whether under our skies or under your own roof dose two–one or de other, or both—have a hand in it. Every one of dem!" was the prelude to his treatise on the matter.)

As for fishing dos-and-don'ts aboard his vessel, his dictates were predictably non-negotiable, though he would take the time to explain them.

On barb-less hooks: The advantage you might gain of less down-time because you unhooked your fish faster and got your hook and line back in action quicker, came with the risk of the fish, on the way in, advancing on the naked hook, slipping it and regaining his freedom. Whereupon it quickly rushes back to the "school" to inform its comrades about the present and lurking danger: Vamos, peligro!. This act of fish intelligence could easily result in them, "toulmundo," picking up and fleeing the vicinity!

This outcome Maas Da-Da dramatized by raising both bulging arms in the air and hurling loud and lusty expletives to the winds!

"Cock-an'-bull story," Patate would hiss to Reb. "Ton-Ton Da-Da jus' cyaan' stan' anyone fishin' faster an' ketching more fish dan he! "Plus, it have anodda advantage to filin' off de barb, an' I-man can show you de proof right here, on meh upper arm." And he rolled back his shirt sleeve to show the shiny, bulging scar tissue on his shoulder. "When fish bitin' like crazy, an' hooks flyin' all 'bout de place, an' de same Ton-Ton Da-Da shoutin'" **'Cyatch de mos' while de cyatchin' is good!'** An' one o' dem hook get into yo' flesh (like happen to me dat time), because of de rush to get yo' line back into action, an' since nobody could put deir han' on a cuttin' pliers at dat moment . . . Hell! Yo' lookin' at de result right here on me uppa arm: t'ree inches of proud flesh, from pluckin' out a barbed hook in a rush! So dat gangrene don' set in lata! So, let de ole man talk he lard oil!

"Well, Patate-Bra, make no mistake: Dis barb business go furda; it gat to do wid different values. It's a Creole/Bossal t'ing! It have to do wid de different value we place on people an' profit margins. Mark my word!"

Patate's position was no less cynical. "Personally, I find de man want to tell people too much what dey could do and cyan't do around here. Once a man know how to fish, why yo' need to get furda into he business? Tell me, Rasta!" Patate asked.

"Like what you talkin' 'bout?"

"You didn't hear de man publicly mockin' me as Fish-barber an' Fish-grooma?"

"Yeah, wat is dat about?"

"Where I learn to fish in meh home islan' every memba o' de crew kyarry a scissors or a small snip, so when he kyetch a fish, he mark it by clippin' off piece of fin or tail, or even shavin' he nose ridge a certain way. Dis way you don't have no argument when de trip ova as to who kyetch what. Because we is all human, and we bong to make a mistake!

Reb listened to Patate's complaint against the skipper, but he neither "brought him nor carried him," as the old folks would say. *"After all, Ton-Ton had a point concernin' markin' fish, which could cause contention an' divisiveness. Besides, when you so call mark a fish like dat, who knows what jumbie trap or obeah you might be settin' for who walk off wid your fish? Especially when you come from certain of these islands!!! (For truth: If I was to tell you some of de nastiness dese people in de islands play on one anodda, it would make your hair stand on edge!!! [I don't need to remine yo' of dem "Put-me-back-where-yo'-fine-me!" story what every one of you hear at leas' twenty times! Ha! But a fella I know stomp de story-man one time when he ask he, "If de real owner so particular, why he doan deman' of de t'ief to 'Put me back* **how** *yo' fine me,' tell me, tell me? De story-man jus' stare he dong fo' a few seconds an' den he answer: 'Sure, anybody could orda anybody else to do anyt'ing, like, Put me back* **when** *yo' fine me! Or even, Put me back* **why** *etc. etc! I leave you to figure out how dese las' two go work!"])*

"And the wrong fish business could be a perfect mistake!!! I'm a positive vibes man! Whichin, I believe Cyap Ton-Ton is too, though we duz have our differences, we born unda de same star. Our birthday is only twenty-four hours apart!

"No! You're crewing on de man boat. De one thing you need to do is follow his rules—even if I-Man mess arong wid de barb, but fo' good reason. Don't give me dat crap about how dey do it back home! Just hang somewhere close to de middle of de school and stay in de stream! Yeah, yeah! I hear you: Middle of anywhere gets you nowhere quick!

"Ha! 'Tis only quickness you worryin' about? Jus' take de time to study how our master fisherman duz bring de school of fish to de boat for de kill! Light chum, heavy chum, in-between chum—till he draw de breakaway renegade away from de school and to his hook. And de renegade, dat's who? Who but you, Patate! Now that he's got you, who follow? We follow, fool! See the mess yo' could get us into?

"And all of this over w'at? You markin' a kiss-me-arse fish which you claim you kyetch! Why de mark and de whole mess I just lay bare for you? Because we don't trus' one anodda! But, in a flash, we'll follow a fool! (If you'll excuse de t'ought!)"

So, on this calm moonlit night, in the lull caused by the tardy slack tide just like that the oily sheen of the sea around them had to have gotten into Maas Da-Da's head. For the stocky light-skinned skipper, standing brim up to his *regular* chumming post at the stern deck, after humming the lines of a bouncy calypso, started to wax lyrical on the cultural amenities of the old days. The times when "You used to be connected to everyt'ing arong you; every place had a name of its own, even when you didn't find it on a map or in a book an' some places even had people or animal names! We even had a number of Follys, Fancies, Hopes, Loves, Jealousies and Whims—dough dose were mostly privileged names for estates owned by rich folks wid plenty lan'; but, dat's anodda story for anodda time!

"And, I'll tell you somet'ing else 'bout dose days—before everyt'ing get so frigging polluted an' overcrowded around here (wid us chokin' on de touris' greenbacks). If you took de time, on a calm, quiet night, Nature might bless you wid de sight of a moonlight rainbow. Yes, Sir! No! I'm not slippin', trippin' or flippin'! I've had dat pleasure more dan once out here on dis Caribbean Sea! Furddamo', t'ings I have witnessed out here on de sea an' could relate to you could fill newspaper pages, if I was a blabbermout'. Like de exact time of arrival to an' departure from our shores of de flock of t'ousands an' t'ousands of laughing gulls in April an' September. Better still, I share *reliable* information; why do you t'ink de visitin' scientists swallow deir pride, haul deir tail in between deir legs an' come lookin' fo' you know who as a guide?"

Was the skipper aware, as he waxed with such delight on that earlier period, that he was dropping his guard, losing a grip on that stoic sobriety he normally and effortlessly imposed in controlling his crew? And that young Reb was slithering towards the gap? And that Patate, followed by the others for sure, would rush in too! ("I perd tête-li! I laché tête- epi bouche-li! He losin' he head, an' he trap spring wide open! Sa sa yé?" Patate surmised in patois and Creole English.)

And that Patate would re-spin a tale of a ridiculous link between the deeper waters he'd fished off his home island and his ability to think deeper than anyone on board! This claim caused an endless polemic between Patate, also known as "Samwekadiw." and the team of elder crewmen, namely Red Bone and Black Mole.

"So, yo' tellin'us: W'en yo' eat a whole fish head—instead of `t'rowin' it away like de Statesida-dem duz do—it make yo' smarta in fish ways? An' w'en yo sarch he head an' even fine an' suck out he eyes . . . an' w'en yo' nyaam he fin-dem, yo' so-called bong to swim betta, an' so on, an' so on?"

"'Tis you who say it!" Samwekadiw, would answer, calmly.

"Yeah. But wait till he tell alyo'," Cyap butted in, "'bout dis pilot cousin w'a he plan to start flyin wid!"

"Den we go got to lissen to story 'bout flyin' high, an' w'at de eye-dem an' wing-dem of frigate bird could do fo' yo'!" Black Mole remarked.

"'Tis da self!" the elders would temporize in chorus.

"He be trippin'!" State declared, seizing the chance to barge into the flow of things.

"Time for a show-down! Fish not biting! Time to organize an' spin real sea-side tales. Enough wid de boas'in an' braggin' 'bout w'a yo cyaan prove o' disprove!" Mole proposed, and he reminded the others, "De bossman said 'no preachin', no judgin'! He din't say notten 'bout swappin' an' stretchin' de trut' here an' dere to keep our spirits up!

"Ah go staat aff wid de story of de soja crab . . . ['Hermit crab, fool,' State shouted.] So, dis fella used to enter de Carnival Parade every year, trus' me, wid a individual production de people call a cultural message.

"Dis year, de message was 'bout de las' whelk. Whichin he said—an' we understand—would lead to de las' soja crab. ['Hermit crab!' State re-interjected. "Soja!" Mole insisted.]

"An' don' make me stress dat hermit is about livin' alone an', chile-less to boot! An' furdda, soja—which everyone know is how we pronounce "soldier"—is 'bout travelin' de world an' spillin' he juice to de four cornas. [**If dis is too coarse, de ladies an' chirren could excuse demselves!**] So dat w'en Mamma soja come down to de seaside to wash, dem t'ousans an' t'ousans of eggs of hers she totin' on her tail is properly laced in soja man-juice. [**Excuse de vulgarity but dis Stateside fool look like he still ain' grasp de difference in how we *see* t'ings!**]

"So . . . to get back to de whelk, whichin everybody know, w'en he depart dis life, he duz leave a shell-house on dis eart' fo' de soja.

"Well . . . dis one Parade, our frien' come down as de poo' las' whelk. Which, some people laugh till deir side ache, but which people on de Tourism an' Taxi Board grumble: 'Dis ain' no laffin' matta! Dis ain' good fo' Tourism; imagine people travel all de way from New York, Atlanta, Orlando, D.C., de mout' waterin' fo a good whelk-an'-rice! Dey go show a visitin' frien' how a real local dish tas'e! An' dis jackass broadcastin' to de world dat Chu'ch out fo' de whelk! Meanin' to say, he light out! O' he 'bout to kick de bucket! Where I come fram, people would beat he wid a cyat-a-nine clear aff de Parade route!'

"But, to get back to de main story . . . de whelk in de Parade had done wid 'bout five years ago . . ."

"An' give t'anks, because yo' tale got too much twis' an' tu'ns," Bone commented.

"But, wait! Ah ain' done! Five years lata, de man show up in de Carnival Parade wid a replica of a giant Vicks VapoRub bottle strapped on to he back. An' dis is de story he relate to de public w'en de radio an' television people interview him 'bout his entry: He used to have dis dream about w'at would happen to de poo' soja, wid all de development an' construction, an' de destruction of our fisheries takin' place on our island . . ."

"Laad, fo Gaad sake, don't go dere!" Bone begged.

"He say, he wake up one maanin', hear de soun' of glass bumpin' an' draggin' outside on de patio, open de do' to see a good-sized soja trackin' along de concrete surface wid a Vicks bottle fo' a shell-house! Exactly how he had see it in de dream!"

To which Bone chose to bless the tale with: "No trut', no dream! Afta all, Marley tell us, No Woman, No Cry!"

Mole was about to follow Patate. But first he must re-impose silence for, he advised them, the end of his tale was too close to the beginning. So, to catch it, they must be all ears! [He forcefully clangs the storm bell.]

"Po' Pa Able bin a mek one table
Step on a loose staple
Get disagreeable
An' cut off he nable!
Bragadam! W'eel ben' an' 'tory en'!"

DOMINOS PRELUDING (AGAIN) ETC.

N**o, no!** No horrific sea monster will emerge from the foul, debris-filled sea water of the Carenage's cul-de-sac, slither over the low bulkhead's rusted casing and work its chaos on the waterfront's evening strollers and passers-by. Though in the minds of these evening loafers it—like a rogue tsunami—could happen whenever it chose to!

No, decidedly! Salt rules! Not just "salt" when, during a fishing event, everyone else is hauling in whopper after whopper, and this one fellow doesn't even feel a pick. *He* is branded "salt."

The salts we mention here are always labeled "Old Salt." Nothing pure about them either; they come soaked in and dripping countless narrative nuances. Better than that, here by the bayside Carenage, where they converge week-nights for domino games— to the last one—they are cast-aside mariners.

So, between moves on the board, they often swap fanciful spicy tales. [And OOPS: "Lady, as yo' head home wid yo' groceries, once more, watch yo' don' swing dose bags an' tumble de bones aaf de board, an break-up a serious domino game!]

That said and re-stated, we return to the high seas with this crossroads business! For if you somehow lost track at this very moment on this Caribbean Sea a tale-telling duel is underway.

Hitch that bluster of yours on to our stories told so far and those to tell, Mister Boss of the board game! ***Yo' hear me good?*** *If you cyan't do dat, den, once again, hold your peace! Give way to omnipresent Effervescence!*

FIRST CHALLENGE TALE

Precious minutes had passed since the clanging of the storm bell by Mole to open the "real" tale-swap, and it was now clear, there was little interest in the Blackout and All-Clear business.

The skipper felt called on to set the tone to the tale-trading, which experience in similar events told him was needed. Absent his guidance, a ton of "bite-an'-blow" trickster tales is all the session would produce the way he saw it.

Regarding this "bite-an'blow" business, Mole pondered to himself: *But "bite-an'-blow" is de upside-down way of lookin' at it, Ton-Ton Da-Da, wid all due respect—afta all, you is de Masta an' fuss officer of dis ship!" But, dose in de know will tell you dat yo'* ***blow fuss, den yo' bite!*** *'Tis not de rat alone w'at duz t'ief de morsel of hot potato usin' dat met'od. De very fish dat we try to trick wid de sweetes', freshes' chum, an' dat we deck our hook smartly wid temptin' bait.*

Dat fish will approach yo' bait, ***blow befo' he bite****, or even* ***blow widout even bitin'*** *while we upstairs here jus' know dat he nibblin'. So, once again, Ton-Ton, meanin' no disrespeck: Get de rule right, whedda 'tis preachin' o fishin', 'tis blow fuss, den bite!"*

The Skipper's choice for an opener, which he believed fit the bill for his Snare and crew, was the one about the high wind, the rustling leaves and the scary hares. The way he'd learned it "in the French School" from a LaFontaine reader, it went like this:

In a horrific windstorm one day a pack of hares, frightened by the violent rustling of leaves on a huge nearby tree, panicked and ran helter-skelter. "Dey run till dey come to a swamp dey couldn' cross!"

"So w'at happen den, Ton-Ton?"

"De frogs in de swamp took to dier heels, springin' dis way an' de odda, in panic too. Why, you ask??? Because dey was afraid dese prancin' beasts uplan' would fall on dem an' devour dem!"

"So?"

"It took a wise old Brother Hare to figure out de puzzle an' to say to his folks: 'Calm down, all of you silly long-eared clowns! Don't you see dat we weren't de only ones dat get frighten! De frogs too get scared out of deir wits over de trifle caused in de beginnin' by de harmless bristlin' leaves!'

"So?"

"'So' you ask? When cyalm was restored among de leapin' animals, wid de frogs finally takin' cue from de cyalmed-down hares dey too stopped prancin' about in de pond. If it wasn't fo' de wisdom of de old hare, de silliness might be goin' on to dis day (since no one could stop de win' from bristlin' de leaves), wid one den anodda set of ignorant beasts takin' to dier heels, wings, fins or whateva out of fear of dey knew not w'at! Even we humans might still be scratchin' our heads to dis day an' prattlin' about it!"

Mole followed up, after first daring to remind the company that Skipper Ton-Ton's story had its merits (but wasn't all that useful, since we were still "prattlin' about it.").

But . . . there was a different lesson to be learned from the one he would tell. It was about a man folks dubbed "the classic Doubting Thomas."

This man found himself at the tail end of a line of trekkers engaged in a questionable enterprise on a beach one dark night. There came a point when the headman turned heels and shouted: "Run for your lives!" The doubter's question, as each one did his about-face and followed suit was: "W'a happen?" To which he got this answer from each one of the prowlers: "You go *stand* dere asking 'W'a happen?' instead of hauling ass like everybody else?"

"So?"

"'So,' *what?* What more does anybody need to know? De wheel ben' an' de story en'. If dat ain' good enough fo' you, try dis: Donkey chew tobacco an' spit white lime!"

Bone (always the loyal backup for Mole) added, for good measure: "Tis one t'ing to be a doubter; in fact, doubting has its place. As ole Nennen tell me one time: Yo' could bar-up yo' door against a t'ief! Try blockin' a liar!"

(Nennen had offered advice of that kind for Reb the day he said to her that he was turning his back on the street hustle and would "try a t'ing" on the sea as a fisherman apprentice: "I understan' meh boy. But look at it dis way: Here on lan'. wid all de good-fo'-nottin-ness dat on yo' track from dawn to dusk, yo' still got neighbas to cushion de blows, good neighba an' bad neighba! Out dere on de seas, w'en de Fury tu'n 'gainst yo', yo' got to go it alone. Every man fo' he'self! But, mine yo', Nennen didn' say don't go!"

"Den, w'a yo' tellin' me, Nennen?"

"OK, if yo' cyaan' figure it out, den, at leas' remember de story 'bout Dolphus!"

"De grave-digga who had plan to hang heself?

"**He**-self! An' notice yo jus' say 'had plan!' De res' is history on dis islan'! Once he kick de stool away, he had a change o' heart! Das when he shout out, 'Neighba, neighba, Ah hangin'! De key fo' meh house. . ."

"On de ledge above meh door!" They chanted together and had a good laugh.

"In case yo' want anodda dose of story-tellin' like dat one but a lot shorter," Nennen gave off (which Reb would loosely share with his mates) "consider how a dumb jackass of a sailor could let someone sign him up to sail on a boat named 'Neva-sail-a-lick!' Could you imagine his predicament every time somebody ask him which port he comin' fram jus' now an' w'at is de name of de vessel?"

"An' now," Red Bone offered, "since yo' bring jackass into it an' his tricks, an' befo' dis tale-swap tumble to de level of cock-an'-bull stories"

"Dog-and-pony, you mean," State interrupted. "That's what we calls them Stateside! Which is a distinct difference from Cat and Mouse . . ., which, given a chance, I could demonstrate the difference," he tried to continue.

". . . dis one is 'bout a donkey an' a deer," Bone blotted him out. "Dese two beasts was forced outta de jungle into de town, by who again?"

"De Park, of course! Aldough nobody could tell yo' w'at crime dey commit 'gains' Man o' any beast!"

"So, dis donkey an' dis deer live on de neighborin' islan'.

"Dese was the largest beasts dat roam de island freely, an' was not totally exterminated only because de local people-dem protest an' complain about ecological an' social engineerin' by de Park, an' some of de strang-headed young ones among dem step forward an' ask: 'Eh-eh! Who nex'? We???'"

The after-hour acts of mischief of these two on the streets and back- and front-yards of the main town, Bone contended, seemed aimed at repaying the conceit, condemnation and condescension of human friend and foe alike! For, no sooner folks on the island went to bed, small families of deer and donkeys made their way into the town and its yards, to chase each other boisterously with ear-piercing shrieks before leaving a trail of havoc from overturned trash bins, mounds of smelly filth and wind-blown debris. (What took place was akin to animal shenanigans at certain reputedly safe and secure public Park sites when bears and racoons wander into them.)-

So, Bone continued, it surprised no one when their disputes ended up with "court-work."

And the accounts, in the form of testimony related in Animal Court, quickly turned into tons-load of moonlight-gathering stories. The one Mole now chose to share went like this:

"Hear ye, hear ye! Len' all ears to dis Commons Court civil case between a wile ass an' a buck deer, presided over by de most honorable Judge Feral Cat, in which each one of de larger local animals lays claim to right-of-way privileges at our only roundabout which in de past was jus' plain Crossroad."

[The story, the teller told, was related to him by a youngish apprentice schoolteacher whose main avocation, he would proudly explain, was a research project on island folk legends.]

Each one of the animals staked his claim for special citizenship rights, basing it on how he first arrived on the island and his standing in the history of this place.

"Who labored harder dan dis loyal jackass an' got mistreated worse?" Donkey asked. And he listed the chores assigned by various bullish masters, and the whippings for which he could show the scars!

"Fus of all, whippings don't count!" Bru Deer interrupted. "An' if dey did, dogs an' slaves and even horses would beat you by far! Get dat straight!"

"Just show me your scars!"

"Order, order!" Shouted Judge Cat.

"Don't challenge me, stubborn Jackass! I bet you dare not ask your noble cousin, Sir Horse to show you his scars! Doesn't he get whipped and prodded harder an' harder, all for a wager? Tell me! But, let's move on! How we got here! You traveled in de hold of a cargo vessel. Dey hoisted you in an' lifted you out in a sling like dey would with a baby in a cradle! Me, with dese spindly legs everybody likes to mock, I *swam* here. You, dey brought here!" Deer repeated. "No one, chased me down, collared an' yoked me, den sold me at de market to de highest bidder!"

Bru Jackass winced from being branded docile and complicit in his bondage condition. He would not dignify the taunt with a reply and merely cocked his long ears, a sure sign that any closer an approach could produce a deadly kick with his newly shod feet to the soli plexus or brittle legs of Skinny Deer.

Their contradicting claims were based on how they arrived on the island, not on who arrived first, of which neither had proof!! But of the two different ways they arrived, one as chattel to labor, the other, due to the runaway development and overcrowding on the main and larger island, and the use of Bru Deer's improbable skinny legs to swim the swift-current channel between these two islands to secure a friendlier habitat.

Magistrate Feral Cat, when it was time to pass judgment, snickered heartily then cited the situation of Rat and his honorable self, and even acknowledged that the latter arrived first, having stowed away on ships (nor did he deny that his and Mongoose's main chore was to eventually check Rat); but that this factor was no longer of much consequence in the Court of Cats. Moreover, while Cat formally was to be the enforcer within households against Rat, as thief and destroyer of goods, as anyone could now attest; this *Island* race of Cats had taken to the wilderness and cherished its freedom above everything else. [For this reason, if you please, he was *honorable* Judge Feral Cat—particularly so titled because he had no known enemies!]

That is, he was of late, if you please, of the league of those cats who wore no collar and befriended rats! Complaints by one side and the other that Cat, under the circumstances, ought to recuse as magistrate for this case were frivolous and a waste of the High Cat Court's valuable time! The Court would recess, and in due time a verdict would be rendered!

Next, the following story was offered by Bone:

A deer one day approached a lion—at a certain distance, of course—and complimented him on his light steps and graceful -gait, especially for a beast of his size! "Who clears the way for me an' my kind? If I had your huge solid size and majestic bearing, Bru Lion, my giant steps would shake the earth for miles ahead of me an' announce my goings an' comings like thunder from de heavens: Make way for Bru Venison!

"However, I trips through the woods an' fields an', if I am noticed at all, the only comment I hear is how swiftly, noiselessly an' breezily I make my way! Dose who say dis might flatter, but it shows me no respect'! You, even with your light an' gentle gait, dey respect and even fear!"

"And in your vain and idle scampering this way and that through the forest, do you ever pause an' think of de utter destruction you do to de hard labor of Ma Spider? I, on the other hand, tread cautiously and, when necessary, back up and take another course forward." During the exchange a little mouse emerged from a nearby hole, trod over to where Bru Lion lay, crawled into the circle on the ground formed by the lion's hind part and tail. She curled up against the lion's warm belly and dozed off in sleep.

"The little mouse that you see this moment, snoozing in de curl of my tail, has earned his peace and safety near me. For by carefully observing Ma Spider as she wove her web to catch a meal and spying on de trapper who knitted his net for big game, she mastered de art of swiftly un-netting what is netted, and untangling what is tangled of course, putting his sharp teeth to good use. And I owe my life to her for rescuing me one day from a hunter's trap! So, Brother Deer, as you cavort carelessly through the woods, take a moment to ponder de labor and livelihood of de small an' delicate Ma Spider.

"If you dismiss this advice an word reaches me of distress you inflict on our friend Ma Spider, the next time you make the mistake of coming as close to me as you are at this moment, my heavy but swift paw will snatch you and then you'll know what it is to really fear Bru Lion's might!"

Mole was next in line, but Bone, anticipating one of his L'il John tales, held forth with this account he'd heard from a priest: "Call dis girl-chile Ti-Janette! Born wid strang African features, an' a corn-row hairstyle, smilin' an' laufin' one secon' an' scowlin' de nex'! An' to boot, she kick her way outta her modda belly! To boot furdda, she already talkin' an' makin' deman's. W'ateva is due de l'il boy-dem is due her. Fair is fair, an' dat kine of mannish boast. 'Lawd have mercy, de midwife cry out! Dis one go make a business outta breakin' man hart. An' she go sure set fire to plantation an' great house. She might even poison her owner! I leave dis one at de foot of de . . .'"

"Ahem, ahem!" Ton-Ton-Da-Da cut him with his reminder.

"I was only goin' to finish by tellin' how de midwife present herself to de pries to confess. Wid her head bow as if she was to blame!" Bone declared.

"Enough, enough! Again, I warn you: Hold it right dere!" Ton-Ton Da-Da ordered. "I already see where dis one is headed, an' again: No judgin' or preachin' on my vessel"

The Skipper's interdiction made Reb grumble: "From meh childhood, I been hearin' stories 'bout Li'l John what born one day an' de next he was promisin' all kinds of magic favors an' gifts to his modda like goin' to de woods, cuttin' down trees, buildin' her a house wid cistern an' flush-toilet; or goin' to de seaside wid a simple woman hair net an' returnin' home wid a basket of enough fish to feed de whole village fo' a whole year! An' so on! An' nobody complain dat anybody was preachin' or judgin'!"

"Maybe so! But remember who was settin' de rules at dat time. I might look like dem who was de bosses, but I hope you know I have different ideas 'bout our dealings wid each odda. An' de blame wall must fall! Period!" We don't need dat rigmarole story 'bout gyurl firebran' an' any poisonin' business, w'ich go' lead to de subjec' of fish-poisonin' w'ich we don't talk 'bout on dis boat, period!"

[The way Ton-Ton Da-Da sees this Justice and Religion business goes this way: Any two reasoning beings ("Mind you, I said reasonin' . . .") facing off, buttin' heads, encounterin' each other on a paat wid room fo' only one to pass at a time, call it what you will, they will argue for dominance, control, to make a point, for the sake of argument, whatever. Den, when dey cyan't settle it? Here comes de Judge or Preacher! He or she will rule for one side and blame de other. Does it en' dere? We know de answer! If argument don't end, an' mos' of de time lead to de rigmarole I jus' describe, den, why start dem?]

Now sensing that this storytelling business might quickly spin out of his reach—especially with that nonsense talk about "donkey chewin' tobacco an' spittin' white lime," State begged the group to just take turns at sharing "back-to-life" stories.

A BACK-TO-LIFE-TALE AT A HAUNTED WRECK

When the subject was raised. Patate at first declared, "Leave me out! I want no part of dat game! Where I come from, nobody—an' I mean nobody—mucks arong in life-an'-deat' make believe! W'en yo' string togedda tales of dat kine it mostly en' up as a mucky "soloup!" But, as expected, State assailed him as a typical stubborn, narrow-minded West Indian; quickly adding that his own father was of the same breed.

Then Patate, to defend his pedigree, snapped up State's bait and explained his reluctance to engage.

In his early days, he tells them as a lone wolf fisherman in his home island of Domalucia, he'd had an experience on the sea one night that taught him a lesson on the hazards of juggling reality and fantasy on the high seas. One night when the moon was in its last quarter, fishing a couple of miles off the coast of his island, struggling against sleep and that imperious boredom infused through slick, gently rolling waves and an unresponsive fishing line, he'd looked up into the skies and started concentrating on the twinkling of a bright reddish star. After a few moments, and many incredulous winks, it simply bedazzled him!

And the following was the outcome from that bedazzlement, he told them: "Dey tell me dat when and where dey find me de nex' mornin', flat on meh back, jus' above de high-water line on de sand, meh tongue was lollin' out, like when yo' pull a rock fish from de deeps quick-quick to de surface. Meh mout' spewin' lard oil in nonsense gibberish; meh two eye-dem was bulgin' like ready to buss out of meh head an' meh limbs was flutterin' like de tentacles of a sea cat or a squid. To dis day, I cyaant tell yo' how I make it to shore! Now I could tell you fo' certain dat de las' t'ought I had t'ink of, was of dat fiery red star/planet inflatin' into a huge globe before meh eyes an' me seein' a squadron of machete-wavin' warriors rushin' out from all sides, headin' to me on dis open sea! An' me, losin' it, cursin' dem, 'Patate Mama-W!' Den, I black out! Dat's de way I remember it, waitin' fo' de bad dream to come to a en'.

"But de fellows on de bay had a different story to tell! Dey decide—an' put it out in de town an' on de radio an' in de newspaper—dat I pull up from de bottom—since de tide had gone slack an' de line had sink to de bottom—dat I pull up, carelessly, a giant conga eel; lan' him in de boat, den let him run me from one en' to de odda of de li'l boat, till out of space, I jump in de water to save meh life!

"Now face de fact! Who yo' go believe? Lone wolf me wid a story 'bout a red star/planet an' a buncha creatures comin' outta it wid machete at me, or a set of lyin', coward an' bad-minded, envious fisherman wid a story every fishin' village on dis chain between Cuba an' Trinidad hear a t'ousan' times 'bout conga eel chasin' man outta boat an' takin' control? Yet, not one of dem could show you de conga dat commit de act!

But de eel story didn't en' dere! De way dis odda fella tell it, I had only mehself an' meh greed to blame. De bank w'ere paat I went to fish dat night—me lone-wolf fisherman—was at a place dey call 'de haunted wreck.' An' I so-call chose it to fish on de sly, reasonin' dat since no one else dare to fish dere afta darkness, it had to be brimmin' wid fish!

"De huge congo eel who live in dat wreck consider it his castle. Accordin' to how de fellas on de bay give de relates—not de ones who say he get me bline drunk wid wine make fram lobsta claw an' lan'crab eye—but anodda set fram furdda dong de bay. Dey claim Brodda Congo grab piece o' ole rope wa he had soakin' in shark brine an' beat me de way de used to do wid unruly children, while makin' me repeat 'Congo is who duz rule dong here! Congo is who duz rule dong here!' An' wid every lash he remine me [So de mout'ogram on de bay say!] of how much time me an meh so-call buddies wid our line an' fishhook snuck outta his reach a luscious fish dat he was trackin' fo' days fo' a meal fo' he, he wife an' de nine pickney!

"De fuss set of fellas had done relate dat Brodda Congo ge so upset at de brass of dis fisherman who come cyatch fish ova he haunted wreck dat he give de line such a haad juck, dat a whole ring of de line on deck curl rong meh body an' drag me strait dong in front of him.

"Once he had control of me, he get me good an' drunk. Den he turn me loose to float up w'reeva de currents and' tide take me."

State shouted a spirited sarcastic "Amen!" Next, he seized the floor to declare brashly: "Some of these strange phenomena bear

commenting on only like a professor would because certain things can only be discussed in a certain fashion! Yes, I hear the choops from my onboard detractors, but here analysis is of the essence. It's what we learn from the dream! Here is the dream I had: I was at the controls driving on a highway with friends. It was a clear day and the landscape was attractive, though not spectacular. Suddenly, "State! State! Staaate!" I was hearing, louder, LOUDER! So, I was coming awake, AND IT WAS ABOUT CONTROL OF THE VEHICLE! I'm now fidgeting with my hands to stop it (though I've never applied brakes or accelerator by hand!) In this instant, a soft voice assures and immediately calms me: 'It's okay! We got it!'"

"So . . .", Black Mole asked, after throwing one knee over the other and leaning back on his elbows, "What was de lesson, Professa Dream Schola?"

"Ha! It looks like even you was jolted awake with that one," State replied. "The point is this much needs to be said about dreams or the back-to-life event; looked at from the inside, it can be layered—or even scrambled! Looked at from the outside, it can be a self-solving puzzle."

Next came Black Mole, after promising extreme brevity. His tale would be found more to the point than any told so far.

It was about an aging dog that fell into a well. His yard buddy, Bro Cat, showed up and immediately wanted to know how the accident had happened. Frien' Dog's response was simple and quick: "Get me out of this mess first, then we'll have time to talk about how it happened later!"

A daisy chain for tale telling had taken form, and the next one told why in the skies two local birds were always at war. And it went like this:

Chickenhawk had just been named "King of the Birds." New on the job, he needed help; he must seek a chief of staff. Busy Trushee was the first to apply. Off the bat, she listed her qualifications: bodyweight, light; soft of step, good ears, excellent memory and gay spirit, not to mention being a hard and cheerful worker and competent spy and purloiner, in addition to tons of other attributes; she clearly outflanked the other candidates.

But, "Tell me no more," growled King Chickenhawk. "Your tongue proves already too loose for the post! Surely, you must be a parrot in trushee clothing! Your chatty babble about your talent tells me that with you as my assistant, whatever should be secret in my government will immediately be broadcast as public knowledge all the way to our far borders and into the neighboring country. Because as you just showed me, you just can't help babbling! Go seek employment as a curbside barker!"

Trushee was displeased and offended with the rejection and went looking for her cousin Chincheree to redress the insult.

Today when you look up into the sky and see a giant chickenhawk under attack from a pair of Chincherees, which are about the same size as the trushee, but twice as vicious, the story goes, they are still trying to repay the insult of the King of Birds to their gabby cousin."

When the tale had been told, Red Bone, not missing the chance to pontificate, cleared his throat heavily, spat overboard and uttered smartly: "A reminder dat what happens on dis vessel . . . no need to say de rest!" The skipper, after a brief threatening look in his direction—since Bone had come that close to crossing the line on preaching—cleared **his** throat and gave one and all to believe that he was giving a pass to the marginal infraction.

SKIPPER'S SPECIAL, THE MOONLIGHT RAINBOW

S**kipper Ton-Ton Da-Da** is far more than a fair-weather, behind-the-helm master of his vessel. He is an expert diver who can report on his personal discovery in deep water of a wreck just off the entrance to the main port of his home island, a wreckage that is home to the richest bank of yellowtail snappers he and most divers in this area have seen! He has also dived in restricted waters just east of a local cay and discovered an unspeakably huge and barren cavern created by UDT dynamite when the Navy conducted secret tests with the blessing of a certain local governor. The displeasure from this discovery torments him no end. For, he will tell you that before the demolition, this spot was the habitat of a great school of hardnose and black jacks that fed a whole village of fishermen and their families that lived near the Careenage.

But his most memorable discovery came not from below the surface but from the skies above. It was the moonlight rainbow. Night fishing alone on these waters, he still beams from this sight on more than one occasion.

Reducing his role to the mere carrier of the tale, he elaborated on his experience with that rainbow against the night sky. For the skipper it was like an overpowering awareness of Man's minimal place within the bubble of the towering sky firmament. At such moments, recalling the almost seamless blend that he'd witnessed between the pallid grey outer band of the rainbow and the field of night blue moonlit sky, he saw himself a Custodian to the dome's majesty!

Ton-Ton Da-Da was certain that none better than he grasped the debt Mankind owed bountiful Nature. "Grey Area, Grey Area, my ass!" he proclaimed. "It's de Pastel Zone! Who needs a pulpit to broadcast this message? If anyone onboard dis vessel, den, exemption granted; let dis vessel be your tabernacle an' temple! An' let someone ring de blasted storm bell like a campfire tambourine! *Say a t'housan' yabbas, even any nappy-dread-lock-haired rebel aboard!"* (The last part he uttered with a mischievous smile. For, mind you, the skipper would remind you in a second that he was a man of no particularly serious religious conviction. Nor was there a prejudiced bone in his body! Although Reb, and even Bone, suspected he had been mucking around in one of those Old Testament books, Isaiah or Job.

(In any case, . . . the ban on the Clergy and the Courts on board still held!)

He studied the reaction of his crew and could tell! The moonlight rainbow business! Hmmph! Was it bewilderment? Was it plain and simple disbelief? Better to let it go before the crew, with their story-telling fangs now sharpened, began spinning their crazy tales on the moon-bow account he'd just rendered. They could only defile it!

Even State might chip in through his bristly baritone with one of his favorites, "Straighten up an' fly right!" Then there would be an argument, and one of them might order him: "Stuff it! Ain' no buzzards or crows or carrion birds arong here! Air too clean for dem!"

"Maybe so, but it's what's behind the story that matters!

(Under full sail, the way the skipper saw it, they would expand on and tweak grotesquely the simple luminary stock he'd cast their way!)

So . . . Ton-Ton could hear the Stateside Black Yankee "duking" through slick improvisations, with the chicken hawk of our skies and the baby mongoose for the original characters: "You see? The scruffy-necked, ugly bird is giving the thieving rodent a free ride in the air. Now, your chicken hawk is tired, and he's fittin' to drop him; your mongoose grabs him by de neck wid his sharp teet' and warns him: You'd better . . .

". . straighten up . . . we know de rest!"

"True, but who gave you the plot, you gang o' kalaloo-grubbing, monkey-chasing, Yankee-hating ingrates?"

"At least, none of us arong here feasts on possum or racoon, though we ain' too sure about Patate, since dey tell me dey feast on manicou where he come from. So, watch your mouth, Mr. Wannabe-Hooker!" Mole warned.

This additional nick-name came from State's habit, when others were catching fish, and he wasn't, to ask, "Hook me up on how to do it, somebody!'

"It's really not all dat complicated," Red Bone said to him once." If yo' eva had to hook-up a bra quick in de dark, whichin you probably had no call unhookin' it in de firs' place, . . . it's de same principle. Now, if yo' lookin' to earn yo' stripes as a rankin' fisherman, yo' fish will be hooked only by de outta lip, an' not wid a hook all de way down in his gill! Same principle, like I said befo'. Yo' press de stud too tight, o' sen' de clip too deep, yo' pinch o' prick de woman sof'-smood flesh! Same way, yo' let de fish gobble de hook down he t'roat! Chu'ch out fo' you! She fine a man less clumsy! Or, de fish eventually bite yo' han' while yo' unhookin' it! Like I alltime say: Everyt'ing connected to somet'ing. Ain' got not'ing ain' connected to not'ing. Tell dem, Bone say dat!"

Ton-Ton Da-Da could see the fine scenario he'd set before them degrading into even a row over what and who belonged (here) and who didn't.

So, he tried once more to shove the tale-session towards neutral territory.

THE SEA BROTHERS, OR MONKEY ROOST

"**Anyway**, talking about places with animal names: In dose days, dose two rocks sitting about midway between two of our main islands, some people called dem 'De Broddas.' Others call de spot 'Monkey Roost,' wid good reason!"

"Now, dis is a story people used to tell about de Broddas, a monkey an' some porpoise. Every seaman know dat porpoise is de best frien' of Man when a shipwreck take place. Dey will come to de aid of a man in de wata, circle him an' protec' him from de vicious shark-dem.

"In dis case, it was a large monkey travelin' with his businessman owner. It was a choppy crossing between dese two islands. De vessel capsize, an' he fine himself separated from his boss/partna an' stranded in de wata. De two porpoises dat come to his rescue didn' have de best of vision an' take him for a li'l boy. No sooner was he under deir protection—even benefittin' from back-rides from one an' de odda—dat he begin a braggin' gibberish about his noble lineage: On de neighborin' island, one of his uncles was a well-known judge an' de other a wealthy politician. (Not to worry about payment for de good deed—though no one had even mentioned de subjec'!) An' so on, and so on. Braggadocci style!

"Indeed? Are dere two broddas anywhere as well known to Man an' Porpoise an' betta dispositioned dan de two you mention?" de porpoise-dem ask.

"None! Absolutely none! How would dey even begin to compare wid de two uncles of mine I mentioned jus' now? Alyo didn' hear me good?"

"Well . . . dese two are! Especially for careless sea-farers an' stranded sea travelers," they told him pointin' to de two nearby rocks juttin' out of de choppy waters. *"An' since you're close relatives to famous broddas, we two porpoise-broddas will just lan' you on dem for safe-keepin' an' lifetime broddaly love!"*

So much for the yakkity monkey who talked his way out of a secure rescue by two friendly porpoises!

"Today, men night-fishing close to de rocks people call De Broddas or Monkey Roost, often report hearin' de over-sized, bodacious monkey jawin' off in de dark between de sounds of de dashing waves harpin' an' screechin' of de gulls, as he flap his hairy arms in de air, tryin' to act like an' talk wid dem, while also tryin' to fly off de rocks like dey duz do. Which he is impossible fo' him!

"But den, it being dat we had other sea places with animal an' people names, if I get any deeper into dat one now, I would have to give a whole string of tales about places wid such names: de Cow an' Calf, Buck Islan', De White Horse Reef, Dog Islan' an' Pup, De Cricket, Duck Islan', De Lizard, De Cockroach, De Ram Goat, De Dogs, Bird Rock, Goat Point, Ram's Head, Turtle Back, Ratta Cay, Bull's Hole, Guana Islan', etc.! Each has its own story!

About this time, Black Mole added words, to a tune he'd been humming under his breath: "Time so hard . . ."

Red Bone, quickly cued-up and filled in with the words:

". . . Daag an' all lookin' work!"

Ton-Ton Da-Da's list was barely uttered before State scoffed back, "Animal names an' animals dat yak an' jive aroun' are nothing new in spinnin' tales when you're among common people in the City! Hell, you hang around certain folk, didn't learn to speak right like I and my folk does, dey call guichi or gullah—some call dem 'monkey chasers; I don't, excep' dey piss me off!! Folks dat came to de City from down souf, peoples that talk mostly like you islan' folks, you'll get your fill of Brer Rabbit an' even Signifying Monkey stories!"

"Oh, yeah? What de hell do you know 'bout de City, apart from zoot-suitin' 'round Harlem like a numbers Don?" Reb asked.

"Zoot-suitin'?" Did you say those words, young Negro? So, you've had a taste of de City and now you're trying to turn historical on me! (And, you, personally, had better watch your mouph, for somefing keeps tellin' me, durin' my City days, I've seen you in suspicious an' shady whereabouts!) But, you're crossin de wrong Negro! Harlem is not my stumpin' groun'; In dem days, I only sneak in and out on weekends to get de lates' scoop on who's planning to overthrow which puppet-string government down your way! (And to pass de dope on to certain trusted federal buddies whose identity might o' might not be of some interes' to de present company!) By 2 am I'm back at Grand Central or Port Authority, headed for White Plains and further norf or Jersey City and points souf!" So, spoke the City man they nicknamed "State," from his habit, during lulls, of singing, whistling and humming the song "New York State of Mind".

The skipper brushed off the sarcasm on the originality of his tales by merely snapping his head up and to one side, while casting on the skinny State-side interloper an icy glare that automatically sucked up from his quarter any morsel of status available on the vessel.

This gesture conveyed the gripe of the whole crew which, piecemeal, went like this: "Dere he goes again wid his City-way-or-No-way! Christ, every time he opens his mouth, it's to tell us that we in in dese islands need to do it—whatever it is—de way dey do it in de City! An' when it's not dat, it's some gripe about somet'ing done to him by some Sol, Paddy, Polack, Guinea, Kraut, Ayrab in . . ."

". . . in de City!" Which came out in unison.

STATE'S SOLID-STATE TALE APPROACH

Ton-Ton Da-Da's reserve of tolerance for State had its own roots; he found that the Big City guy possessed useful knowledge, especially about motors and gauges, things of that sort; hence added value as an on-board quick-fix engine and equipment troubleshooter.

(State had done a couple of years at a southern A&M. And he had his own theory on the main cause of malfunction in motors, which, when given a soapbox, he extended to vital processes in living entities. *If hydraulics or deficient amperage is a suspect in mechanical glitches, then faulty life-"draulics,"* he advanced, *is often the culprit in malfunction where human health is concerned.*

The way he viewed matters, if one could reduce problems in electronic flow to issues related to ohms, amperes and voltage, those related to fuel flow in a system to issues of pressure, vacuums, syphoning and contamination, then—just as easily—one could extend the logic to our feeding practices and the nutrition process, which then linked directly to belching, farting and fecal elimination!

"Chittlin' o' caviar," he declared, "hot foul air or crap is de equalizer!" This, all in one breath! But State's laws of bodily physics didn't end there. He shared with the crew his conviction of the unbroken link between dream activity and dauntless physical challenges.

As a fledgling tennis player, he had struggled with the serve, which fellow-players ridiculed as "pyaw-pyaw." But, happily, the battle came to an end after a dream he had where he extended his arms and neck in a way he'd never done before. He emerged from that dream and suddenly could serve as well as the best of pros.

And since the Serve dream and its outcome coincided with a period when he was being challenged by days of flatulence in his bowels, and another embarrassing debilitating bodily dysfunction, he came to fancy that the same psycho-bio-dynamics could apply in various fashions and circumstances. One only had to dream hard enough about it. Continuity did the rest!

It could even work for erections! Bingo!!! Forget about Viagra and Cialis!! The only problem would be, how to trigger the magic dream!

Yet, the chips and scars on his psyche from that extended term trapped in the City's beguiling cultural grid, boxed into his City College student role by protective [e claimed!!!] *West Indian guardians*, hardly facilitated a good mix with the others aboard. So, his rants on *life-draulics,* when not un-noticed, were laughed at.

In any case, State, with his expertise and usefulness established, was a lesser concern to the skipper, since he wasn't likely to find a cohort for any mischief he might concoct, having no known natural ally on board.

SEEDS OF A COMPLOT?

For, while not an overpowering preoccupation, there was this peevish pondering of the skipper about a potential challenge to his authority, and from where?. (Competent and confident fishing skippers "grow" an immunity to the skeptic among their crew; the one frig of a doubter who always knows a better fishing hole or sounder baiting technique!)

Still, Tranquility (his "bottom line") was bound firmly to Security! And the two young Caribbean border-liners—more than any other crew— the way Ton-Ton saw it—might just butt heads to present a threat to his peace of mind. And the ringleader would be: Who but the "Rusta"! (His buddy, the skipper surmised, was nothing but bluster, with his looney claims about being the deepest thinker aboard simply from fishing in greater depths! This boast, in any case, had to be tampered lest it acquire a life.

(It was Red Bone, on authority of Seniority, who countered the borderline theories of State and SamwekadiW:

"So . . ., den we're to suppose dat the fore-day cooin' of de mountain dove durin' full moon means de mating of de pair will produce super doves?" And, Black Mole, second in Seniority, piling on with his tale about a pair of blue pigeons he'd spied on, mating on a Good Friday. "So, accordin' to your logic, Samwekadiw, de pair were practicin' 'free love?' For, it is well known in our tradition dat Good Friday eggs don't fertilize!")

What, a complot? Under my nose? (An' to t'ink: this confounded Rusta dey call Reb, from what my contacts tole me about his street work for de downtown Party Machine before he came to Sea the Bosses were to make of him a black carbon-copy of me!

Nooo! Any hint of a pact between these two younger crewmen needed to be rendered asunder. Right away! If you eavesdropped on them, their private mumblings and prattle might cause you to view them like "chamber pot an' bottom."

Such were the prior thoughts of Maas Da-Da, in more lucid moments!

More recently, though, he had downgraded the complot threat and somewhat turned it on end, thinking more along survival lines: If it's leadership you need, put the young rebel in charge of the all-essential bilge-security detail! (Down there he'll occupy the lowest and murkiest bowels of the vessel! However, he will execute a function only below that of the skipper! Let him puff his chest on that concoction!)

As for his sidekick, Samwekadiw (aka Patate), who bothered to pay him any attention, with his insipid claims, most of which fell in the class of tallish tales, the latest one being about a friend of his who had trained a pair of frigate birds to swoop down on a bonito or mackerel caught on a trolled line, snatch it from the hook and bring it back to his boat, to increase his catch . . . da, da, da. Moreover, he had even offered the one about a bird-charmer who had trained his rooster for more efficient and civil courting and mating behavior whereby he dropped that well-known sideways strut and instead sought out the hen's beak for an extended pecking act before climbing her back to plant his seed!

In a charitable mood, the skipper would glaze over Patate's outrageous claims by advising his crew: "Envy no man for knowledge he got or how he get it!"

"Get or got?" Black Mole quizzed.

"What de hell difference it makes?" Red Bone asked.

With concerns about mischief from the two younger men for the moment in part laid to rest, Maas considered his sea-going fortress secured on the three most significant of fronts: Bone and Mole covering intelligence and wisdom, while providing a communications guardrail; State for mechanical trouble-shooting, and the "rusta" as bilge-bailer chief, in the unlikely event. . .!!!

[Take time/tick time and Yabba-pot a yabba!]

A BIT FROM MAAS DA-DA'S PARABLE KIT

P***ssst***, *reader! You know by now that many stories are told during this time on the high seas. And Ton-Ton Maas Da-Da's presence in these bouts is at times pivotal.*

But, his contribution to the storytelling events is seldom dramatic or extravagant; his tales dare to edify and gently editorialize, often leaving a hint of correction, while not tripping on his own judging and preaching ban!

In fact, his was a stock reply to prods from the crew for input in a storytelling séance: "Heads up for the Take Time/Tick Time/Time Bomb from me or the Yabba-Pot-plabba from you-know-who! (You choose which!)" Then, he might relate a tale like the following:

One day returning from a good fishing trip at a distant bank and, in a mood to share the bliss, he decided to look in on the notorious Skipper Bully. This colleague had retired and of late was something of a recluse not so much through his own choice but largely for roguish and generally vile behavior towards neighbors, which in turn led to banishment from the company of decent folks. Tagging along with the skipper to Bully's house on the distant north shore was Lindy, an easy-going, soft-spoken and harmless crewmember.

Bully welcomed the two into his modest living quarters. But, no sooner, had simple Lindy crossed the threshold and been introduced to him than the host grabbed his walking stick from where it hung on a wall, hooked it around Lindy's neck and dragged him to one side, while announcing gleefully, "Jus' de man I was waitin' for . . . to try out meh new beau stick!"

"And, how did dat visit en', Ton-Ton?"

"'En'?' You asked! Life for de notorious bad bull of de Seas an' Lan' damn nearly en' at dat moment! It take all de force I have in dese fingers on meh two han-dem, to separate Lindy clench han-dem from de man t'roat!"

* * *

It wasn't always easy to tell where the skipper's sea-taling ended and his rule-making began. If you asked crewman Black Mole, (who expected one day a promotion to Sexton at the Cathedral) the skipper's credo in these matters, he'd gathered during a tiller-side chat, was sustained by his personal take on Isaiah's words on Jesse's Rod and acts he equated with "burying de hatchet," as he had heard them from the pulpit during a Lenten mass many years ago.

ON RAYS "BREACHING" AND TURTLES "BLOWING"

D**is-barbing** a fish hook in Ton-Ton Da-Da's book, was a serious infraction, and it signaled insubordination by the dis-barber. For, the intent was clear! The sighting of a turtle popping its head out of the water, however, was another matter! The impulse to announce before anyone else your visual trophy might be uncontrollable. Yet, Skipper Maas had his rules! If one popped his head out of the water, and you saw it, you were not to say "Turtle!" You could make signs to someone, point to the beast, mimic his swimming motions, etc. But don't call his name! People said it had to do with a tradition about turtles bringing bad luck to fishing trips.

"Okay, Ton-Ton Da-Da, but what about de sting ray leapin' out of de water?"

"Night an' day! De ray leaps to fart! De turtle surfaces to exhale his stinkin' breat' dat he's held so long under water! Which could have to do wid his foul mood by de time he reach de surface. Wid de dark spell he'll cast over yo' fishing trip! Yo' ever look him in de eye?

"Besides, if you know anything 'bout sperm whales an' dat ambergris stuff dey release when *dey* breach; a chunk of deir stinkin' shit dat yo'll fine on a beach in deir neighborhood brings you tens of t'ousands from de perfume industry!

"Who is to say what dey might learn about ray poop? Den, one day we sail right under de breachin' fartin' ray dat's got de runnings, collect a payload of his shit! After dat, no need to fish any more fo' de rest of our lives!

[***Take time, or tick it etc!***]

ONE WAY SECURITY TRAFFIC ON GANGPLANK

And now, (the required formalities and paperwork—above and below the counter—executed), Dixie Island Gal leaves the east bay of our western cruise port, cheerfully more buoyant from the disembarking of her boisterous cargo of 200 pleasure seekers, curious enough to invest 100 clams (miserly on-shore pocket change, as the custom goes) in fantasy-filled quests into the remotest nooks and crannies of the cays and promontories that dot our offshore perimeter.

Her day's work done, she's heading back to her protected place between the mangroves, in the Careenage where she moors upon a well-earned peace each night.

Presently the horde of tourists she's just spewed unto the dock are gathered by two Industry-decked young, fair skinned stewardesses and are being steered back aboard the 4000-passenger cruise ship docked a few hundred yards to the west of the ferry wharf. The lady stewards dutifully bring up the rear where they can best conduct vigilance against alleged and highly *profiled* poachers and snatchers of items worn, but more importantly keep their eyes on venal matrons and aging male skirt-snares bent on that last fling before re-containment in the bowels dubbed statehouses of their floating metropolis.

Upon crossing the gangplank each returning tourist is scrutinized by Security against the smuggling aboard of Island contaminants like weapons, drugs, Island animal life or other unsavory items.

Interestingly, on the initial crossing of this very gangplank (in the opposite direction early this morning) no one checked to see what or how much of the above or related items these folks might be transporting to and dumping on the island!

When the subject of the selective treatment of tourists at the entry and exit points is mentioned by young Island militants, among whom Reb is routinely lumped, this contradiction calls forth a fiercely defensive response from loyal Government operatives, and they first scoff, then preen and finally brag about it as a model of Hassle-Free Tourism.

"Sure, ignoramuses and miscreants like you will raise hell about Government sell-out and corruption. That's because we succeed in seeking you out and containing you and your kind away from our visitors, when we could and should instead be mowing down even the least toxic of you. The way they do in most banana republics! Yes! With the stinking weed you keep bootlegging to decent visitors and citizens, ruining this destination's proud and noble name!"

FROM THE CAPTAIN'S LOG

Our first encounter with DIG was the night of the near collision.

[The above notation and what follows herein are based on the words of Skipper Maas-Da-Da, who scribbled down the original version in the vessel's log, in keeping with local Maritime regulations.

[The jagged uneven scribbling appearing in the original draft of what follows leaves no doubt about the writer's hesitancy and calculation before committing this information to his on-board log:]

While this entry might well upset some official authorized to review this report, and even if, as certain higher-ups like to warn, "there could be consequences," in view of current user conflicts in our crowded and stressful island Maritime industry, documentation of the incident in question,[which is hereby re-transcribed for the sake of clarity, as the original writer faced various spelling and grammatical challenges] ***about which I, pro bono (as a concerned citizen) am hereby doing my part,[which I hereby underscore]*** *merits serious scrutiny:*

On that night the tour vessel or ferry seen frequently in these waters bearing the name "Dixie Island Girl," presented herself through the foggy overcast, and, after first circling our vessel, the Snare, and entering and traversing the chum slick of a craft legitimately engaged in float-fishing, Dixie, approached the Snare on the windward side, literally butting and cuffing our vessel so violently as to rip loose several feet of rub rail.

Skipper of the vessel identified himself—without so much as offering a polite greeting—and announced they were delivering said vessel to the Islands. Got lost. Hadn't a clue where they were. Begged your humble servant for a bearing and to be put on course. Especially since he had been warned about reefs and non-functioning markers close to their destination. Who would imagine that after their rude-arse conduct on approach, your servant would render the service requested!

Or that the self-same Dixie would eventually become a thorn in my side, by regularly intruding on and disrupting my regular and vital fishing activity!

Now, this part-owner and skipper, yours truly, knows well the digs of Dixie, in the Careenage, behind a spit of thick mangroves, and could easily, under the cover of darkness, exact Justice! Especially, given the numerous intrusions of said vessel—even brazenly during daylight hours—and her many companion vessels—into my boat's legitimate fishing space and activities over a considerable period of time, just so their touring passengers might obtain close-ups—and what they call "photo-ops"—of our fishing practices. ["See natives boating their catch!"] That close they approach, we can hear them on their PA system!]

But, being a law-abiding sea-farer (furthermore, true to my own "no judging, no preaching" credo), I leave this matter to the Higher Power! (I have to add here that the younger rebels in our population that we like to scorn and condemn cannot be all that wrong about the double standard practiced by the authorities in these matters. "No justice, no peace!" they declare, and it have merit and deserve due consideration!)

Submitted in lieu of spoken testimony, for the record!

Master of the Bossal Snare

ALERT: SLICK PLANK ON TO WOBBLY VESSEL!

***F**ish* *not biting? No sweat! [**Yabba pot etc.**]*

Reb recollects more words of advice from the aunt everyone called Nennen:

She was a kindly but severe taskmistress, with little tolerance for tomorrow-ism who seemed always to urge him on:

"Never mine certain people prattlin' about odda people's natty-head dreadlocks an' lifestyle an' your I-man way of talkin' when you feel like it! Always remember: You troubled no one, an' what didn't meet you, didn't pass you!" (Thinking of it now, it must have been her way of saying:

"Get over it!" Even: "Put behind you dis confounded concern wid de Crossroads an' its roogoodoo!")

Well, she no doubt forgot what her own mother, his Granny, had told him one time about things that happen there—at the Crossroads—at the stroke of midnight on certain full moon nights: "Dey—mostly light-skinned werewolves, but also a few Black an' Mulatta jumbies, amongst dem—dey frolic, dey romp, dey tumble! An' den—if you get caught in deir presence, like under a sudden rain shower—dey growl so loud, you stop in your tracks, squeeze your t'ighs an' buttocks not to pee yourself or mess your clothes. Much, much worse dan de t'reatening mumblin's dat you hear comin' out of Maya Hole when a storm is brewin'! De row an' roogoodoo at de Crossroads is much worse!"

He ruminates further:

Besides, why, when calamity was in the air, did older women, after fanning the fold of their dress between their thighs, always state: "Look at de ***cross*** *dis is for me!" And even this Patate Mama-w, the fisherman fellow from Domini-Lucia, my onboard occasional sidekick, when he finishes one of his boastful relates, why does he always say, "****Cross*** *my heart,* ***Kwaze*** *tcher-mwen?"*

To boot, (and Nennen, doesn't know this!) a retired chef on an island schooner-trader had related to Reb one day that a man died while they were making their way between Macoris in Santo Domingo and St. Thomas. "An' we tack back!" he said. "Tack back?" Reb had asked 'Yeah! Dat was de custom! A man dies, you change course right away!"

Another detour-filled Sea Crossroads? Who knows?

"De sea-cook who told you dat is a confounded blasphemer! Our Lord an' Master don't play dem type of games, tackin dis way an' de other, w'en your time come!" Nennen would say, if she heard the story.

Well . . . not everything Nennen said, you could find in writing. For instance, she used to say of someone she would call a reprobate: "He is too blasted redempted!" Look it up as Reb did, in the Dictionary, and search for it in old Court records, he has not located that word!

Was it "redemptive" she and others who used the word meant? Quién sabe?!

"But, it's not 'passed you,' Man!" Daniel, a hi-school buddy—less radical than he— would insist. "It's crossed you! It's de crossin' business you have to watch out for!"

(And, now that he gives it further thought, maybe there was something more to this passed/crossed toss-up than met the eye!)

"Whatever!" he would respond, depriving this doubting Daniel of the endless argument he'd started salivating for. "Why waste my breath!" Especially when he remembers that every other member of the class in those days could agree that: "Nothing beats a trial but a failure" said pretty

much the same thing as: "Nothing ventured, nothing gained," while this imbecile insisted that the right way to say it was: "Nothing beats a failure, etc., etc." Then why waste time with his *opinions about anything?*

So, let's move on! (Although, if you wanted to split hairs, that crossed *for* passed *just might be right!) Hmmph!*

Yabba pot a-yabba!

THE PLOT POT: WILL IT BUBBLE? OR . . .?

Dear Reader: So . . ., you've held fast through the meanderings of these tales. And so, our narrator feels pressed to share with you the following very personal observation:

So now, here's a trick a tale might play on its teller: Somewhere in the telling: you might barely blink, it might effervesce prematurely! (Excuse the bookish choice of words! (We know, you gave it a pass earlier!) "Boil over" or "explode" just won't cut it!)

And, if it manages to (Ahem!) effervesce on you, you can never quite get over the suspicion of having missed that very first bubble when it broke the surface, and therefore you cannot suppress the bothersome belief that Security, during your shift, was deficient!

Yet, the bubbling event, hardly more noteworthy normally than a working man's after-lunch belch, will have had the good effect of giving "air" to the text on hand, a feature all our readers, we trust, will find—or are finding (Ahem, again!) —beneficial. (Which . . .ahem . . . explains. But does not excuse, the present ex-cursus!)

Hence, . . . away with stuffy, corked-up, monotonous accounts of seamen tale-swapping aboard the Bossal! Meanwhile, keep your sight on the two adversaries aboard that played a role in significant events. And notice how the forces verbalize, namely through the mantras ***"Yabba pot a yabba"*** *and* ***"Take Time/Tick Time/Time Bomb."***

"To what good end these utterances," the reader asks?" "Simply," our narrator and scribe responds, "They pre-course and herald incidents in the

ongoing verbal, though often muted, combat between the two principal characters, both holdovers from the historic period in our islands of unprecedented political lapidation (although arrogant and lazy chroniclers would score it bookishly as de-lapidation.)"

(In case, the reader wonders why all this to-do about so little, let him/her be advised that, in like fashion to the way that first bubble must break the surface before boiling can proceed, fresh air—not to forget water especially in the present circumstances—is at a premium for the tales' healthy gestation and nourishment. Wasn't it the late Hugo Chavez who, several years ago, at the podium, in the UN, famously held his breath, sighed, fanned away the stuffy air and asked the doors and windows be opened to let **out** a certain stench, and let **in** refreshing breezes, at the outset of his historic manifesto on or about some New Order?)

* * *

Now, on this crossroads business, since maritime cartographers routinely designate "roads" on their charts, be advised dear reader (though you would have guessed it by now) that crossroads—even if only graded as mere crossings when on the sea—have had their role to play (often even a "tipping-point" one) in our relates so far. So . . ., don't underestimate certain Spirit-driven content, laid out above—and some of them obviously missed—in Crossroad-linked events. Hence, again, the **Yabba pot a-yabba, Take Time/Tick Time/Time Bomb** mantras**,** in service to the ever-essential Effervescence!)

So, you ask (impatient and increasingly distracting and, as such, distracted reader): A sprinkling of tales that have to do with fishing, fishing craft and fishermen (or told by the latter, already universally known for their license on untruths) here driven to boot by the turbulent currents at the X-roads??? Well . . . Well! So, what?)

Yet, the master of the vessel Bossal Snare, the fair-skinned and stocky Ton-Ton-Da-Da, having arrived at his personal career Crossroads and having made a miraculously secure exit out of its swirling political riptides, through a decision forged early in his life, and having chosen his path—a categorically apolitical and irreverent one—decisively, he now basks within a bubble of security at least on his vessel, bolstered by the armor of the three simple vows he imposes at the outset of each trip before the "good-to-go" could be declared and vessel and crew could sail forth

This safe zone is further secured by the 3-fold grid of Bone and Mole (for intelligence and wisdom), State (for technical trouble-shooting) and Reb, aka "Rusta," (for bilge safety).

The obvious first rule was an old maritime interdiction, and it addressed approaches by one boat to another on the high seas; the second forbade preaching and judging at sea. The third one was, as one might have expected, the universal ban on mutinous conduct.

As for the last of the security details in place [And it is so obvious it barely merits mention]: If it was a fishing vessel, it was meant to perform and function *on* the water; certainly not *under* water!

The blow struck by the whale shark to the Snare's hull and (presumably) steering and propulsion units was cause for concern, and the skipper immediately ordered an inspection. Because the engine was shut down at the time of the shock, compared to getting shut down from the shock, it was only speculative to measure the full impact of the lash from the sea beast. Yet, a small pool of water was already visible through a checkpoint manhole undoubtedly from one or both stuffing boxes (notably, the first for the prop and the second for the rudder).

Stuffing boxes are notorious sinkers of boats! To start the motor and engage the propeller as a test of the damage was to run the risk of producing a gushing leak at the box. As for the rudder, better secure the steering wheel to prevent swinging this way and that! Such was the advice from State, the Snare's trouble-shooter.

Perhaps . . .??? Well…better leave that aside! The Snare would be better off waiting to be towed (by whom and when??) to a haven. Such was the thought process of Skipper Ton-Ton.

Reb, ordered to conduct the bilge inspection, discovered a much ampler space below deck of the round-bottom craft than he had imagined existing. To the point that he quipped with the fellows afterward that "Ton-Ton could hold a banquet down there" if he wished! He now also could better understand how "below deck" of some people's vessel could get gutted during a search by enforcers! (Little did he know how useful this information would be an hour or so later!)

A PURLOINED MANGO FOR STARTERS

There is a fundamental element of risk and uncertainty that stalks even the least significant of sea voyages. Capricious Mother Nature gets the blame when most mishaps take place.

But, what about the Master of the Vessel!!! His moods and disposition, from one moment to the other, have notoriously been linked to *which side of the bed he exited on* any given day!

On the day Captain Maas Da-Da came close to setting forth

without his fishing ace the young and enigmatic Rasta Reb aboard, not for a moment did the younger man blame it on absent-mindedness. Nor, had the departure taken place abruptly, would it have surprised him if there'd followed an about-face and a return trip for the pick-up! Such was the evolving nature of the relationship between skipper and junior mate aboard the Bossal Snare; the messaging-flow between the two was uneven and complicated.

On the day in question, as it turned out, the exit from the bed had nothing to do with the skipper's icy disposition; the gripe had really to do with a purloined mango from the man's grafted fruit tree (an event that has been mentioned earlier).

* * *

Now, just a minute! How did we get here, anyway??? Tell me!

Why, we *swam* here, Friends! For, the clash was inevitable; (In the background, the two vessels had been on a collision course for an indefinite period. Our best sages, griots and cultural gatekeepers had issued warnings of an impending collision from time immemorial, but no one paid heed. The casualties would be numberless! Yet, who listened? Tell me!)

Many perished during the Crossing! Who knows: the debris you will find—if you wait long enough—especially in the wake of DIG (short for Dixie Island Gal) along with her cohorts, as she continues lumbering on, oblivious, through our seascape, eroding with her bling-bling splash, pristine beaches and uprooting millennia coral beds! Crimes "their" hired minions and agent publicists would vehemently accuse the Bossal Snares of our seas of committing, when, it is well known, the only visits the Snare (and its companion vessels) made to those beaches was for the purpose of collecting a few bags of sand for chumming and for the seining of fry bait, such as could be found anymore!

Take the time to solicit Skipper Maas Da-Da's checkered view of Dixie Island Gal! He shrugs: "What's dere to say about her? Bossal is a simple fisherman vessel. DIG is a bling-bling frigger-woman craft! Period! An' I speak from experience: De aggression of dat rude-arse boat de day of de first encounter!!!

"De massive hulk approached my boat and gave her one hell of a broadside shove **on de windward side to boot!** Dat should have told me something! Like: neither wink nor blink if you want to know who is runnin' t'ings or what time it is arong here!"

THIS BOSSAL SNARE NAMING ISSUE

As for Reb, his main gripe had to do with a lot more than the barbed hook business. The vessel's name pissed him no end. "Bossal-Snare! W'at kine of bomba/loin claat name dat is to give a boat?

Well . . ., there's a story behind the naming of the vessel, Ton-Ton Da-Da used to explain.

It all went back to when he and his partner purchased the 50-foot lobster boat in Newport, Rhode Island two decades ago. The aging skipper they'd bought her from had begged one small vow of them; in re-naming her that they, in one form or another, retain the word "Snare." (Aboard this vessel, he declared, he'd needed no fish finder or other fancy electronic tracking device! He bragged to them: She finds the fish on her own!

"Or, the fish finds her round-bottom backside!" his partner had quipped behind their backs. *"Let's wait to see if our simple-minded, warm-blooded fish are in the know!"*

"OK, but snare what, or whom?" Maas had asked, *pro forma*.

"Bossals or Maroons!" The partner had offered, (taking excessive license with the seller's simple petition.) Then he added, "But I prefer Bossals. It includes all those African savages who've resisted the boss civilization the rest of us have accepted as ours. So, that's it! We'll call her the Bossal-Snare!"

Thus, the seller, unknowingly, had played his role in the *tour de force* of the co-buyer's cynical longtime chum, a retired commissioned officer.

"Spice it up!" he'd argued, knowing full well the meaning of the noun and the irony he was injecting into the boat's title. (For him, the act was of no more consequence than, say, adding the image of a peg-legged, one-eyed pirate type to a label for a spice sauce from Grenada or rum from St. Croix.)

"Bossal-Snare! Bossal-Snare!" Reb would re-rail one day in a fit of outrage. "W'at de bomba claat kinda friggin' name dat is to give a boat? Dese people good wicked, yo' know! Dat's why de bredren an' de sistren call dem Babylonians! An' de wrath of Jah . . . jus' give it time, hmmph! Fo', nobody cyaan't tell me dese White and mulatta-Creole folks ain' muckin' arong in our culture an' disrespectin' our cultural heros! First of all, de name too long an' insipid. 'Insipid,' but I still say, it got some wickedness behine dem putting dem words togedda! I am warnin' one an' all: Jah don't play. Jah will have his way!

"Fo', everyone know," he expanded, "when dey use de word bossal, dey referrin' to dem of our ancestors dat dey t'ief outta Africa, dat once dey lan' on dese islands, dese same captives had de courage to take to de bush an' den by hidin' an' sneakin', spyin' an' sackin', hittin' an' runnin', bunnin' an' pillagin', bringin', an' cyarryin', you name it, dey lead us outta Slavery! Jah Bless! Pshaaw! As if Bossalism was a common crime like Vandalism or odda Babylon misconduck!"

"Culture Vanity an' her poor cousin, Culture Disconnect will, be many a man's . . . excuse me, many a people's downfall," Reb would quietly pontificate, and he would prop up his position by asking: "W'at kinda just-come buckra build his balcony directly above Main Street, an' for w'at reason?

"New money! It give de owner w'at he'll call a clearer view of *the human condition*, an' let me say it now: For de common man, de parade pass an' de dogs bark! After all, isn't dat how

Black-Out, Air-Raid an' All-Clear come into dis picture? Check out de thumbed-up noses of our hoi-poloi in de face of wartime heroism an' its casualties! Class games of ingrates! Pshaw!"

While Reb entertained such thoughts, parallel ones cursed through the mind of the ship's master.

Only minimally known to these two main adversaries and crewmates was the fact that, during a good part of their lives, they had coincided and even crisscrossed each other in their journeys through the island's political minefield.

And now they were face to face and engaging each other on this fishing vessel here in the Caribbean. Drifting towards who knows where! Free-birds they were, but also effective exiles from the normal social labyrinth of their land cohorts.

A SHARED STINT IN THE POLITICAL CAULDRON

Ton-Ton Da-Da's arrival on these islands, listed as possessions of the United States, though officially not part of them, from his home island two hundred miles up-the-chain coincided with the emergence of a new politics of reform and public policy experimentation, namely one closely linked to the transition out of "plantocracy," on the larger, more profitable island of this territory, and "emporium fever," on the smaller, more accessible and less arable one. On both islands, as was the case throughout the region, the overarching policy and political driver could best be described as applied "emporia-ism." (The reforms in question had their variants on all the islands of the chain. Moreover, far-fetched as the reference might seem, the rise and fall of the notorious Idi Amin, as related in Kapuscinski's *Ébène: aventures africaines,* lays bare the cynic game played by colonial powers as they ceremoniously withdrew from their holdings and promoted "independence," while substituting an even more draconian ruler-ship under contrasting guise and hue!)

Residual commercial and economic interests of the former bosses always trumped the exuberant egalitarian fantasies of the local folk.

Fast on the heels of the exodus of these masters of land, industry and commerce, there entered through this busy corridor the corps of facilitators! Call this one a pimp, the other a puppet, the third, a go-fer, the fourth an informer! Does it matter the label? The French refer to him as an "entremetteur," and the Spanish—especially if it has to do with access to women— a "chulo."

At its noblest, the dispensers of the magic tokens and rules would target high officials like ministers and governors among the newly "independents." At its basest, it entrapped the minions of those actors, the local petty self-proclaimed bigshots!

The outcome, throughout these former colonies and possessions, is the automatic installation of puppets and stooges as replacements for entrenched colonial rulers. What was unique in this case was the US component. For, pressing hard on the heels of the local buckra class—European initiated and acculturated—in its exodus from the landed gentry niche was a band of roughshod, no-nonsense southern American entrepreneurs, a brand of owners and bosses that did not hesitate to offer the advice to an underling or neophyte foreman: "What is needed around here is the whip and the promise of a noose to get things moving the way they oughta!"

The approach of the emerging "local" political class went like this: "This fellow—the light-skinned one— looks more like them than he or they look like us. Plant him in the middle of any dealings we have with them! No way to go wrong!"

This situation provided the ideal entry point for an arriving adventurer from another island, especially with the cachet that the then twenty-odd year-old Ton-Ton Da-Da possessed: ruddy skin pigmentation, a generally robust appearance and the cultural accoutrements of an *education* "in the French system."

The situation during that time, was the following: Island-White (known as buckra) plantation owners and Main Street merchants were anxiously taking flight and, in so doing, cutting their losses in the face of a depressed "liberalized" economy; these folks were lighter complexioned people with prefixes to their name like "van", "von", "de", "du", "mac" or "o", and suffixes like "sen" or "son," or plain "s."

With their withdrawal what was left was more than a breach in the previously well-functioning economically productive system; a critical cog had failed!

At ground level a new polity was taking shape, a critical mass that bore freshly and horrendously etched on its mind the utility of matches, kerosene and a torch (sometimes plus a well sharpened machete) in forcing survival concessions from employers and Government alike.

Thus, the groundwork had been laid for the paths our two shipmates would travel, though separately, to gain significance and value in this island community. Their experiences took place two decades apart but rather mirrored each other.

Ton-Ton Da-Da's recruitment for "go-fer" services to the emerging political machine happened during the period when the island colony was transitioning from Europe-driven plantocracy and emporia-ism to "wanna-be" American republican democracy.

Reb's undercover/informant role with the Enforcement authorities emerged hardly a generation later. Even so, that role was largely derivative to the rapid urbanism and societal splintering that attended the dismantling and re-configuration of the islands' cultural canons. In that earlier time and framework—as one example of a gaping fault line—Correction and Castigation were quick, decisive and irreproachable.

The new cultural mode and mindset called for responses to infractions and criminality that were more tempered and judicious—when not simply muted—that the young miscreant quickly learned to manipulate and subvert. Ask the average senior Culture-bearer his or her opinion on that period! "Dat was de beginning of de en' of respect an' order or respect for order! Turn an' twist it whichever way you wish!"

Not unlike the social accelerators that enabled Da-Da's smooth entry into the vacated go-between slot created by buckra class flight, Reb's baggage of Street-sense and acute survival instincts, honed mostly during his New York City "student" days, placed him among the top candidates for informant/mole and convenient provocateur among the youthful rebellious and marginalized crowd.

The recruiter needed only to keep a sharp eye on the portals and byways of marginalized youth on the island to wager confidently that Reb could fit the bill! (His bona-fides of knotted locks and barreling gait were his badge of utility and service.)

Almost overnight the role of "entremetteur" took on critical importance in island politics and hence in Public Policy. Listed on the Government payroll roster as a complaint officer or neighborhood liaison was an individual who could wield critical powers on who got the job and who got the pink slip. While some quibbled about this new and costly layer of political clout, especially as it evolved towards at-large provocateur and informer activity, a certain erudite and esteemed leader and jurist gave gravitas to the legislative body of the day and its machinations by referring to them as a hybridization of the Westminster and the American models!

It is in this modus operandi that the rocky and complicated liaison between the two mariners across two to three generations now functioned and found validation.

Thus, even if on the surface Maas and Reb have carried on like adversaries to the bone, they were possessed of a comrade-at-arms bond that had been forged in that incredibly efficient island cultural and political furnace; a key credo under girding that process was "Half a loaf is better . . .!" One learned, formatively, to gnaw away at the purloined and prized morsel by blowing first and then biting, as the thieving rat does.

Even as both men fulfilled their own gateway roles in the political grid-work that ran the islands' affairs, they found various gaps, weak links and contradictions that their superiors and absentee masters would have preferred go undiscovered.

For, a careless move by the manipulator could spark a major social crisis or evolve into remnant dogma which could be cynically subverted by simple folk of the underclass.

Reb had once asked a Stateside waitress about the fast pace of the service she rendered: Why were she and her co-workers rushing about the task of serving and bussing tables at such a furious pace, "like crazy ants on a mission to transport and warehouse the carcass of a roach or centipede?"

(For, in his Big City experience he had learned of practiced and principled work slow-downs!) Did these people's bosses have them under surveillance, and at the end of a day could show them video proof of why they would be either retained or released the following day? Her response was: "Shush! I think they've got an eye or a camera and mike on me at this very moment." (Might not even such a brief exchange as this one, at critical moments in the impending and inevitable clash of interests, one day, yield bountiful complicity? Driven, to boot, by a romantic adventure?)

The note he left on his table said, in capital letters: "THIS IS NOT SERVICE; THIS IS MORE THAN TOILING; THIS IS SERVITUDE. I LEAVE THIS NOTE AFTER HEARING A CUSTOMER OF YOUR OWN ILK ASK YOU IF IT'S A WHIP THEY APPLY TO YOU GIRLS. BESIDES, IF YOU COULD SEE THE BACK OF THAT CUSTOMER'S T-SHIRT! THE LOGO SAYS: "WORKERS RIGHTS ARE HUMAN RIGHTS!"

In like fashion, during a conversation Ton-Ton had once with a Black laborer in which he endeavored to explain John Bull the black man had cut him short: "DE WAY WE SEE IT ARONG HERE: IT GOT BIG WHITE BULL AN' BIG BLACK BULL! NOW, YOU TELL ME WHICH ONE IS DE ONE TO FEAR DE MOST?"

When Skipper Maas ***th***ought back to it, the rapid riposte of the black tradesman seared a raw nerve, and he vowed within himself come hell or high water the following thoughts one day he must share with his on-board Pan-African nemesis:

"De vessel's name was a bone of contention with you from de get-go! An' you were right to take issue wid it! I am not an ignoramus on your people's history. Bossal means 'Saltwater African' or a still untamed and untrained slave. That name was given the boat by my malicious partner when we traveled to New England to purchase and take possession of the craft. Some cockamamie notion he had where he saw himself on the bow, heavin' a metal grain at a big black sea beast of the Caribbean! A piece of Moby Dick madness!

"But . . . his craziness, that came from too many years in the US military—or maybe buckra arrogance! You came aboard, and you had odda issues! Issues about big and little dogs dat certain people not only let into their house, but also allow to crawl into bed wid dem; de double standard when dey t'row dat football player in jail for fightin' pitbulls, but have no problems wid whipping de shit out of a filly to win a wager, or t'rowing two men in a ring to batter each odda's brain to a puree. Listen, I heard your grumblings about justice an' fairness!

"Mine you, it wasn't in shackles dat yo' come de 'board de Snare!

"As for me, I come to this islan' as a young man, not in shackles either! As buckra as dey come, but especially a penny-less buckra, if you ever saw one! Certain political an' commercial interest seize upon my usefulness as a go-between. I had de light shade of skin like dem, but de language an' style of de real locals! An' my credentials was impeccable in dat sense. Dey used me well to beef up dat *status quo* empire of diers an' to put aff de day of reckonin. which we all know has to come!

"You, on de other han', lef' dese islands in yo' formative years, travel to de Big Apple, got exposed to an' dabble in Harlem style radicalism an' dat radical buy-Black-ism! Return to dese islan's with a fire burnin' in yo' chest, a flame fo' change!

"So . . .take out your scale of justice an' your fairness calculator an' tell me if we don't have a few scores in common!

"An' one mo' t'ing! Dis wise an' jolly Nennen or Granny who give you advice 'bout quittin' de Street racket an' shippin' out to Sea, she know a Jesus Christ t'ing bout de Sea trade? Dat out here 'tain jus' 'bout right angles an' de wrang ones! Dat w'en yo' navigatin' out here, dependin' on de conditions, yo' got to pinch aff w'a yo' get, an' work wid dat! Wedda a complete circle or a strait'line—an' everyt'ing between one an' de odda! Yet an' still, yo' did de right t'ing in pickin' her brain! Out here on de sea, w'en t'ings get rough an' turn upside dong yo' need a chink to prop up yo' brain. Even if 'tis only by *t'inkin'* of Nennen wid yo issues wrap up in a kerchief an' tuck between her breasts fo' privacy. Or, if it is too much of a load yo' give her, stuff in a bundle an' set on a katta on top her head!

WHAT ADRIFT IN THE C-KRAAL COULD PORTEND, OR WHO SAID STOCK IS GIVEN THAT YOU CAN JUST "TAKE?"

S**uch** were the moods of Skipper Maas that at times he would take a moment to commiserate and even laugh at himself, his predicaments and his surroundings. During these fishing trips, it was at Unda de Cyalm, flat on his back on the transom's curved deck, that such introspection took place.

Yet, here they were now, not Unda de Cyalm but well adrift in the middle of the night on an unpredictable Caribbean Sea at the height of the northern storm season to boot.

Time to take stock! But . . . take stock of . . .???

In assembling a crew, for instance, apart from attention to how he recruited his senior security detail, his was the simplest of vetting procedures. It was as though beyond the initial contact and interview he allowed his instincts to sniff out who qualified to sail with him. To some extent the lesser the load the freer the soul! No tiresome cross-exam and the lighter you were when you showed up the better was your chance of sailing.

Take stock? What do I know, for example, about who can swim, and who can't?

About the two older men, Red Bone and Black Mole: the first reported that as a boy, some older fellows had cornered him one day on a jetty and tossed him off, to "swim or shit!" The second one said that, his granny, knowing of the common "older boys'" risk, had forbidden him to go *anywhere* near the water once they were anywhere around!

As for the remainder of the crew: who knows? Patate with all his bragging and bluster about deeper waters and deep thinking, what's to be made of that? Besides, does this clown know that his view might be turned on end to support the bizarre libel of Blacks as non-swimmers, backed up with loose claims about buoyancy and purported top-heavy-ness?

With State and Reb, their special utility came essentially through an article of faith, and their practical value for the trip's success overshadowed the question of whether or not they were natural swimmers. Besides, they made a good fit; their roles in the scheme of things and issues on the high seas were simply etched out in the Skipper's modus operandi. They were stop-gaps against misadventure at the technical and mechanical levels.

And State was the vessel's tech man-of-business.

Your anchor? Like it said in a hymn you learned even as a child, your anchor should hold. And it *held!* At first, anyway! Normally, there's enough rope and chain to go 300 feet deep.

But, here and now, because of the mischief of that confounded cross fish that, after getting hooked, peeled off hundreds of feet of the 40-pound hand line, allegedly wrapped it around the anchor chain and hoisted it loose, just take a whiff of the pickle! Though, this outcome could also have been the result of faulty scoping by the crew man assigned the chore of setting the anchor! Whatever the case, it now *dangles* insipidly above the floor of the Trench on its hundreds of feet of scope.

TALES TO HASH AND TALES TO TRASH

Yessir! What a swarm of yarns they'd cast into the Basin's night firmament! Some tales were worthy of hashing, and some of trashing!

For one crew member what was particularly memorable was the one about sting rays breaching to fart. Another crew had amused more than bedazzled the rest with the claim he thinks deeper just because the ocean floor surrounding his home island runs deeper than that of his neighboring islands! Still, another crew man had a tale about a mongoose and a chicken hawk, promising to look out for each other's little ones, with a deception of one leading to loss of all the offspring of both. Then there's the one about the frogs who got pissed because the log given them as a ruler was too passive and lacked pride of stride. They complained so loudly and for so long to the Man Upstairs that he finally gave them an egret, who devoured the better part of the race of them!

The fellow who used the words "Patate Mama-W" to swear would have his mates believe that he had a neighbor who succeeded in teaching male yard pigeons to be spurred and fight each other in a pit.

Yes, miracles happened, and one heard stories of surprising outcomes to shipwreck, such as the one where neither skipper nor his lone mate could swim a lick, but both had survived a shipwreck, by each one clinging to *his* half of the broken vessel till they landed on the rocks that wrecked them in the first place!

Then, there were other happenings that challenged common beliefs going way back!

But (at the end of the day, as the saying goes these days), it is here also, Unda de Cyalm, where, about ten hours earlier, just before dusk, miles to the southwest, on the horizon they'd spotted the authorized and despised villain! Of course, they were in a trustworthy haven—as the name of the spot implies—but the creepy vision on that line between ocean and sky had stirred up thoughts in Ton-Ton Da-Da's mind of an Enforcement raid on a friend's fishing vessel that had gutted it to the state of a hapless and useless shell! (Protestations to the local authorities produced nothing but a deaf ear and a blind eye! A response well known to him, when he reported encroachments by the fleet of bling-bling tour boats now infesting his favorite fishing banks.)

Ton-Ton Da-Da, once charged up by his anger at the Enforcement forces, could list multiple cases of questionable priorities. "Intercept a li'l fisherman an' his crew on a everyday fishin' trip, to put bread on de table an' feed a starvin' village; disrupt dese po' folks makin' somet'ing outta dis life; tear asunder de interior of de vessel. An' what about dat excellent fishin' bank for hardnose jacks just off Buck Islan' dat de frogmen, wid de approval of a postwar island administration, had turned into an underwater wasteland of uninhabitable caverns wid deir dynamite charges! All de while claimin' dese exercises an' experiments were vital for National Defense! Hmmph!

BUT, W'AT DID DEY DO WID DAT SAME GANGLIN' DANISH STEAMER W'AT WAS BROUGHT HERE AN' MODIFIED ILLEGALLY TO RUN CARGO ON DESE SAME WATERS? (For, everybody knows, de new owners had removed de ballast tanks to create more cargo space for a bigger payload, outta pyure greed.) NOTTEN, NOFING ELSE! YO' CALL DAT KINDA ENFORCEMENT JUSTICE? DE OLE FOLKS SAY: PAPPA DON'

LIKE UGLY! Dat is why as, was the consensus of de crew, it was a surprise to no one de day w'en dat long steamer had to face de music . . .and went down jus' pass Round Rock wid her full load of Christmas cargo.

With relish they took turns telling and re-telling the story: Play hide-an-seek between the string of cays from Puerto Rico up to the BVI. But when she met the open Atlantic and had to turn broadside, if only for a few minutes, flip right over and went bottom! "Bragadam!"

Ton-Ton's anger over selective enforcement was such that he proclaimed loudly to his crew: "De day dese fellows raid my boat and find drugs or weapons stash anywhere on it, is de day I will head straight to my known competitor and enemy on shore, an', believe me, he go have Hell to pay! Fo', I will know dat he had to have somet'ing to do wid settin' me up! An' even if he didn't, de innocent will pay fo' de guilty! It wouldn't be de fuss time dat happen!"

NOGGIN CHURNIN' WITH C-CRISIS LOOMIN'

When the navigational lights appeared through the fog, in the distance, Skipper Ton-Ton Da-Da's mind, hopping and skipping smartly out of the Unda-de-Cyalm reverie, quickly processed a series of scenarios and outcomes: The most fanciful was: Could it be the Dixie Island Girl was on their tracks yet one more time, all the way out here, on this God-forsaken ocean, at this unfathomable hour? (For DIG seemed destined or programmed to cross their paths whenever and wherever.)

Then, abruptly and clearly, it wasn't a dream he was having (which would at best be a re-run of the view he and his crew had had earlier in the trip, while moored at **Unda de Cyalm**, of the Enforcer patrol vessel, snaking along the murky horizon, waiting to pounce. An event that brought back into sharp focus that recent boarding of his friend's vessel and the demolition of its interior—all for not-to-be-found illegal booty!)

No! He was not in a dream!

A vessel was in fact approaching them through the thick fog as they continued, disabled, to drift, with its navigational lights mysteriously glowing then dimming and disappearing only to cycle again in reverse order, at intervals of forty or so seconds. (The mystery, for the skipper, was short lived; after a moment he called up his experience in vertical floating and figured out how a strong undertow could gently rotate a body and create this peekaboo effect; it was no doubt this rotating action—this twirling—that was toying on his own vessel with the peekaboo effect.) If the approaching vessel was the DIG, Maas quickly figured, there would be no throwing them a rope (or even accepting one from them and hitching up.) No setting them on course either! (With such dubious bearings that he possessed anyway at the moment would it matter?) Let the DIG even if she was bursting at her beams with blasé visiting pleasure-seekers (with their bundles of greenbacks destined to local pockets and coffers) fend for herself; find her own exit out of this probable shared calamity.

Skipper Ton-Ton Da-Da would not deny a personal gripe against the touring ferry group and company!) For, he'd seen so many sides of the Industry and its impact on public policies and on the life of the common man! The deference extended to them in those public hearings was one thing. But then, as a mooring neighbor just off the new Liner Dock and Tourism Terminal, he'd personally witnessed the dawn-to-dusk hustle-bustle for survival of even the pleasure-boat operators, and he'd drawn his own conclusions. Nothing the big sharks in the Industry demanded (particularly the owners and operators of the mega ships) was denied them.

"Dredge our footprint in your harbor and two miles seaward ten feet deeper for the next hyper-megas under construction at this moment in the Norway shipyards, or forget the next year's ten visits to your port!" "An' whatabout our local fishermen?" "Das who you worryin' about?" asks our just hired Liaison Officer. Then he answers his own question: "Befo' you know it, he'll forget how to even bait a hook, but be an expert at cyatching every greenback dat de new touris liner scatter in de air!"

Besides being a mooring neighbor of Dixie in the Carenage, Maas had his sources in certain backrooms and the corridors and lobbies of high-end port restaurants!

And, if behine dis train-wreck collapsing on de backs of poor local folk, dere is an argument about regional politics an' safe investments an' alliances—an' I've heard enough of dat garbage in anodda life, as a water-boy for de Machine politicos—den, why not take your repulsive greenbacks an' bless the strugglin' Cuban peasants wid dem? Or de Dominicanos or de Haitians? Excuse me! Scratch de last two groups, for even I can see, dey're much too black!

So, why even announce an' hole de last volley of public hearin's on local fishermen's traditional sites an' rights, in de face of concessions made for wider an' deeper lanes into an' out our ports. So, what if a gang of Rustas appear at a hearing dubbed "Cultural Tourism on the Move" protestin' an' disruptin' the proceedin's, smellin' de rat poised to infest de next parcel of land' dey were plowin' fo' survival food!!!

De Rustas had every friggin' right!

Offensive and disgustin' as dey is, sometimes, wid deir raids on people's mango trees an' blarin' claims of Jah Bless, because De Most High authorizes dis an' commands de odda!

But right is right!

To expand on this point Ton-Ton offered the following scenario from the Past, then asked his crew to tell if at times right is not wrong:

"Here's dis little finger of a main bay you've known most of your life as a haven from de high winds an' breakin' waves on de open channel when t'ings turn nasty out dere; a sudden squall or gale. It's so safe an, quiet dat people around here even call it De Krik [for "creek"]. You rememba as a boy enterin' it an' rowin' all de way in. Dat's where you fine yourself facin' de tallest grove of giant mangles you'll find in dese islan's. *No, no!*

"No use looking for dem dese days!

"I'm taking you back to when we were young bucks, borrowin' Uncle's rowboat, learnin' to navigate an' fish in dese waters, returnin' to shore an' first visitin' our special Krik. Dere, t'ree, fou', five of us in our li'l rowboat, could part de branches de way you would a curtain, enter dis shaded retreat of clean, clear water and curved mangrove roots. An', once in dere, give vent to your wildes' fantasies: about girls, dotin' elderly family members at gatherin's, events like schoolyard brawls, mischief of an' towards teachers, an' so on. Talk about a sanctuary fo' de buddin' mariner!

"An' today, what's left of it! Dey—de ones who tell us dey're super conservationists—dey mowed it down an' plow it under. Today it is de offices an' reception hall of de Conservancy! Conserve w'at??? Plough unda centuries-old mangroves! Hmmmph! Can dis ever be right? Haven't countless generations of de island's young mariner dreamers been deprived of dat safe haven?

Ton-Ton had thought fleetingly of the DIG but wasted no time considering the scenario of her falling on them.

"Out of my life, Dixie!" he told himself. "I'm handlin' w'at's beneat' our nose an' loomin'!"

The skipper's prudence has a long reach, though most seamen adrift are known to welcome whatever comes their way from land-in-the-distance. Be it a soaring wayward seabird or a soggy piece of driftwood! So, even if it was what looked like spooky lights in the distance, who is to tell if it wasn't just that! A spooky mirage good only to build up your hopes!

Reb, in the meantime, bogged down on the "bossal" mockery and effrontery in the naming of the boat and his inability—despite several wheelhouse tête-à-têtes—in convincing Ton-Ton Maas to gracefully accept the tag "buckra" the way he himself had come to live with the skipper's open and repeated references to him as "rusta." "You call me 'rusta.' Everybody else call me 'rasta' fram my attachment to

Modda Africa! No big deal! We refer to you as 'buckra.' It's not you in particular; it's your people! OK? We're squared now?"

Still, it's only with a long face that Ton-Ton Da-Da lived with the buckra *brand* that crowned his persona in these islands and that kept him at all times in a state of high social alert. How many times he'd had to remind those that crewed with him and other Island social contacts: "I am as West Indian as any friggin' man on board or on this islan'!"

ABOUT HUNGER BOLTS AND A PUNGENT SUSPECT CARGO

Men of the sea down our way will tell you of hunger *bolts* (*Pangs* are much less intense!) happening far out at sea, with no land (or other vessel with an active galley) anywhere in sight, when of a sudden the distinct and pungent aroma of a Caribbean goat stew—the Dominica/St. Lucia sailor would call it a "Colombo"—or daubed pork, overtook their senses of smell and taste. Ton-Ton, given to light philosophizing from one moment to another, would call up the "safety" sign he'd seen on rigs in the States: "If you can't see me, I can't see you." And, he wondered to: "If I can smell you, etc., etc." But then, again: Who eva see or hear about a sea vessel wid rear-views, stickin' out like a pair of ear lobes! An', if dey exist, den dey could only exist on a Enforcer boat . . . or a Drug Lord boat . . . or on a Park boat! Tryin' to make sure deir back is covered!

But then again, what de hell. . .! Stay de course!

In the present circumstances, was it one of those head games being played on our skipper by his senses—or, might it be the earlier idle babble about crossroads as commerce and market sites which are always so impregnated with the gritty odor and dust of raw spices and roadside cuisine? So that now, suddenly, there settled on his mind the disturbing conjecture about cargo aboard that could attract the attention of the Authorities through its odor, and that could complicate matters for him!

"What is not on the manifest," old mariners quipped, "belongs to the captain!"

So, there could occur this encounter with our potential rescuers, the way Ton-Ton envisions it, that's going well so far. The Authorities come aboard, promising a "routine check."

"Check, check; no problem! By the way, Skip, what's the scent I seem to be picking up, kinda weedy?" Skipper Ton-Ton continues to imagine how an encounter with the Authorities could start heading south. And it could happen! After all, these fellows board your boat as crew. *You've hardly delved into deir "when-evers" and "where-evers." An' with dat maroon an' bossal survival business so deep in deir head, God alone knows what mysterious "currutle"—like a charm, some Congo root or some wisdom-spirits—dey might be bootleggin' aboard "jus' in case!"*

And now, that the fog had lifted, clearly any interception in the making had nothing to do with the Dixie Island Girl! The potential visitor/intruder was a large patrol craft. Whose? You couldn't tell!

No, sir! A high seas search must be avoided at all costs!

Just so: Master Maas shouted the order: "All hands, below deck! Rustaman, you lead de way! You too, Black Mole! Go! Red Bone, you stay!"

Now, when the skipper shouted that command, especially since the order was directed firstly at Reb, the reader might wonder if something went awry in this report (communications between these two being what they were—mostly a sustained stand-off.)

Yet, the young Rastafarian—and his followers—complied on the spot!

So . . . what had begun, the day Maas almost cast-off, almost leaving his crew on shore, as an indirect slur on young "rustas" as mango thieves, had, of late evolved into a lot more than a clearing of the throat, accompanied by a coarse hawking and spitting-out of bile between grunts of "Rusta dis, rusta dat!" There were now signs of healing. (And, at times, the two even pow-wowed amicably at the helm!)

The original rub had to do with much more than Reb daring to dis-barb his fishing hooks! By the time Maas Da-Da stormed onto the boat fuming about the raiding of his grafted mango tree by the band of "rustas" the "t'ing" between them was far more than a mere "throwing of words." The message, looking his generic culprit square in the eye, was, "Here is what I have to say to you an' yours:"

Even so, in interesting ways, these two are comrades-at-arms, had a common history of playing and even besting the Island political alchemy. Not to mention: their birth under the same star!

In time the two would stand on common ground!

RESCUE SANS SECURITY

Instead of the DIG that they had come to expect would be the intruder into their uncharted but now personally familiar sea-space, the large grey vessel that emerged from behind the foggy veil was in fact a military ship of undetermined nationality, supposedly on patrol.

A direct encounter with the Authorities was as thick in the mind of the skipper as the fog that had veiled the Navy ship's approach! And Reb and companions now understood better the Skipper's order to disappear below deck.

For, the big ship's appearance immediately brought to their mind (besides the misdirected interdiction and rummaging of a certain fishing craft (oft mentioned by Skipper Ton-Ton Da-Da up to very recently), a sea-going account from an acquaintance named Mac the skipper had even more recently shared with them; it went like this:

Adrift on a barge he captained for delivery from Curacao to Santo Domingo, that craft and crew had been sighted by a navy ship of unknown registry. No sooner the spotlight had targeted and approached them than the loudspeaker blared: "On deck, every last soul!"

"Yo' cyan't be serious, Mac!" the skipper had asked his informer.

"No? W'en me an' meh crew complied wid de orda, dat spotlight square us up in even sharpa focus, an' den we hear de loudspeaker blare: 'Strip to de skin, every last soul!'"

Mac told Maas, that that was when he knew what it meant in Slavery days to be an auctioneer's pawn and stand there passively while

Massa and cheeky Missy gawked over, touched and patted the product in their most private places in the Public Square.

The voice on the loudspeaker eventually informed them that towing was not an option; their position would be reported, and relief be sent. Which did happen! God bless! For . . ., a tug did show up later that day, with a friendlier crew (men that looked more like and sounded more like Mac and his crew.)

They were towed to a friendly haven where (for some unexplained reason) a man none of them had seen or known of before presented himself and provided resources and assistance for the needed overhaul and repairs plus the wherewithal for the return trip home for his slow, cumbersome cargo barge.

Skipper Maas Da-Da, as stoic as ever, commenting on the unpleasant interlude and the fortunate outcome for Mac and his barge people, and not giving any ground on his edicts on preaching and judging, simply characterized it as "a happening of what had to happen!"

Reb, on the other hand, had tried his best to link the rescue reported by the skipper to some vague Crossroads miracle but finally "let it go" when he realized his Nennen was no longer around to assist in unraveling the puzzle.

What remained undisputable among all concerned was, Maas was taking nothing for granted when, in response to a potential boarding by Enforcement officers, he had given the order: "Every man below deck! You, take the lead, Rustaman! You stay, Red Bone!" That command, they agreed, was the essential tipping point in ending the suspense and drama of this fishing trip.

And, given everything that had happened on the trip, including tales shared—many of dubious merit—, the command had really surprised no one.

DEN . . . TON-TON'S NOGGIN UP 'N' WENT JOGGIN'

It was where a key event of this saga started, namely the theft of a mango—in the shade of the prize grafted fruit tree, bearer of the fateful purloined fruit—that Red Bone and Black Mole, retired fishing buddies and former crewmates aboard the Bossal Snare, adepts at the "say one, say two" taling gambit, sometimes stopped by, neighborly, to chew the fat with the sea-logged and brain-fatigued Skipper Ton-Ton- Da-Da.

Truth be told, these visits barely registered with Ton-Ton. His spouse, a gentle, caring Puerto Rican woman, approaching four score in years, with increasing frequency and a dash of impatience, (since she'd warned them that the words "rusta" and "coast guard cutter" were verboten) would, hush-hush, point her index to her right temple to signal her mate's mental lapses. (In our vernacular, this registered as "He crack! An' it's jus' 'roun de corna fo' you!") Still the two dropped by, as faithful sea companions and reminded him of "de magic you pulled off when you placed de "rusta" like you called him in charge to get de crew below deck? In fact, when *you* put him in charge of securin' de bilge even earlier! Especially, since de two of you was always haulin' an' pullin' an' couldn' set horse! No, you don't have to answer! I am jus' saying one to say

. . ."

"Two," Mole would jump in. "Fo' true! After de way you an' Reb were at each other like cat an' dog most of de trip . . . yet, if you say one . . . you've got to say . . ."

"Two . . . De genius an' stroke of luck in dis is: Befo', w'en yo' sen' de "rusta [Excuse de mention!] to check in de bilge fo' leaks de Snare receive from de whale shark, de young man discover space we neva knew exist below befo'. De perfec' hidin' place for us from dem snoopin' busy-body officials. De fine jus' you an' Red Bone aboard. So, dey neva look any furdda!

It was from this habit of call/responsc, back and forth, tit for tat, say one/say two, dis an' dat, what have you, between Bone and Mole, that they came to surmise in end the, the coming full circle or running the gamut of contention, connivance and complicity between Skipper Ton-Ton and Ras.

Dis all put togedda, yo' could call:

"A Creole-Bossal-Buckra Culture (Con)Fusion."

Finis

EPILOGUE

It took place in its entirety within the perimeter of the Caribbean Kraal. It opened with the force of a massive tsunami-like ground swell . . . It hurtled forward and struck, then backward it meandered seaward like the desperately bottled note of the hopelessly brain-baked shipwrecked sailor. It closed with the improbable rescue of a cranky round-bottomed fishing vessel and its motley, tale-spooked pan-Caribbean crew.

CPSIA information can be obtained
at www.ICGtesting.com
Printed in the USA
BVHW031211050319
541824BV00008B/122/P